Winter's Tales

NEW SERIES 10

Winter's Tales

NEW SERIES 10

*

EDITED BY

Robin Baird-Smith

Constable · London

First published in Great Britain 1994
by Constable and Company Limited
3 The Lanchesters
162 Fulham Palace Road
London W6 9ER
ISBN 0 09 473830 0
Set in Imprint 12pt by
CentraCet Limited, Cambridge
Printed in Great Britain by
St Edmundsbury Press Ltd
Bury St Edmunds, Suffolk

A CIP catalogue record for this book
is available from the British Library

CONTENTS

ACKNOWLEDGEMENTS

EDITOR'S NOTE

This year, the new series of *Winter's Tales* celebrates its tenth birthday. But this annual collection of short stories goes back much longer than that. *Winter's Tales* was first published by Macmillan twenty-nine years ago. In 1985 Constable launched this new series.

The criteria for inclusion remain the same today as they were at the beginning. The stories must be original to *Winter's Tales*. The collection is entirely eclectic – it avoids that current obsession, a theme. It delights in including writers of all inclinations, outlooks and ages. *Winter's Tales* has never been exclusively traditional, experimental or avant-garde, though in each volume there are stories which fall into these categories.

From the Publisher's point of view, the most exciting thing about *Winter's Tales* is the discovery of new talent. The authors whose work appeared in *Winter's Tales* and who then went on to become successful novelists are too numerous to name. In recent times, however, mention should be made of Paul Sayer (Whitbread Prize Winner), Peter Benson (Guardian Fiction Prize Winner) and Robert Edric (James Tait Black Memorial Award).

Ad multos annos

Robin Baird-Smith

ADULTERY FOR BEGINNERS

Clare Colvin

By the third year of our marriage the all-enveloping presence of my husband had permeated every atom of my being. Not even a brief phone conversation escaped his scrutiny. As the receiver clicked he would call out, 'Who was that? What did they want?'

If I coughed when I was upstairs in the bedroom he would shout from the sitting-room, 'That's a nasty cough!'

If I left the house for the corner shop he wanted to know where I was going, what I would be doing, how long I would be. And why hadn't I got the cream when I was doing the big shop-in at Sainsbury's?

It reminded me of the little boy in the verse who wouldn't let his mother go down to the end of town alone, but it was rather less charming and its effect was disabling. I began to read books designed to tap the market of women with low self-esteem – there was *The Woman Who Loved Too Much*, *The Confidence Trick*, *The Doormat Syndrome*, and finally a book entitled *Are You Under Control?* It was divided into three parts, 'The Controlling Parents', 'The Controlling Husband' and 'The Controlling Self'. I turned to 'The Controlling Husband'. I could hardly believe that Richard had not taken instruction from this book, so closely did it describe his behaviour, which the authors said was intended to reduce the wife to a puppet. Did Richard know what he was doing? Should I buy this book and read it aloud to him? I bought it and when he asked what I was reading I quoted a passage.

'Psycho-babble,' he said.

'It describes you exactly.'

'Absolute bollocks. All those writers are doing is preying upon inadequate women. How much did it cost you?'

Richard is an architect, which means he controls the lives of people who don't know that he exists, though they may feel the influence of a malign being as their bodies collide with three-piece suites that are too large for their 15×12 sitting/diners. He is of the Toy Town school – a style he defines as a reaction against brutalism, but it is only brutalism in a new form with red bricks and perky enamelled balconies. The inhabitants' quirks of personality are ironed out, in an equation of space versus cost. Richard stands over the finely drafted plans and the models of estates like a god looking out over creation and seeing it is good. He is the Great Architect, no less.

Such is his authority over the way people live their lives that he has become a pundit, writing articles for newspapers on the interrelationship of architecture and behaviour. I long for the inhabitants of Toy Town to start throwing bottles at the police from his enamelled balconies, but they don't because they have been crippled by their mortgages. They take the bottles down to the recycling bin instead and feel a glimmer of satisfaction at the sound of glass breaking as it hits other bottles.

We, of course, live in a Victorian house overlooking a leafy square. If you suggest inconsistency, he will say that in fact his architecture takes in the classic principles of town squares. The only difference is that the trees have not had time to establish themselves. Nevertheless, our Victorian rooms could accommodate two Toy Town sitting/diners, even four where he has knocked down the walls. So many walls in our house have been demolished that the only private space left is the bathroom.

'You were in there a long time,' he calls up from the

sitting-room. He has not moved from the sofa, but his voice projects up the well of the stairs, resonating against the sanded and polished treads. When I hear his voice I can see him in my mind, feet up on the sofa, Saturday supplements spread around him. He has, or had, a clean-cut profile that is now a little blurred, the chin's sharpness softened by calories and years. His complexion has a permanent reddish flush that contrasts with the blue of his eyes. The eyes of a martinet, someone once said. It will be no surprise to hear that our sex life is desultory. It is partly my silent resistance to the invasion of every other aspect of my being, partly the desexing practised on wives, and colluded in by both, which renders you sexually invisible, your wedding ring a Tarn-helm. In *The Denigration Game*, Dr Miriam Pfeiffer says this is because a sexual wife is a threat – she may demand satisfaction when the husband is not up to it.

So here I am, a de-sexed, non-threatening wife being taken out to dinner with his new client the Ministry of Arts from France. Richard's articles have been translated into French and there has been a glossy spread in one of their architectural magazines. Momentarily thinking European for 1992 and bypassing their own people, the Ministry of Arts have commissioned the Great Architect to create a Toy Town arts centre, with space for opera, theatre, galleries, cafés and trampolines.

We are sitting at a circular table in our favourite res-taurant to which we have taken the man from the ministry and his young colleague, studying the menu at varying distances from our noses. Our favourite restaurant has white tiles on the walls like a public lavatory, but the food is good and you are given to understand that you are part of an élite by being there. Richard is sitting at my right, the young colleague, whose name is Bruno, is on my left, and the man from the ministry, René Leblanc, is opposite. Leblanc has a high complexion and dark polished hair and everything about him shrieks Paris at you. Bruno is a tall young man who looks as if he needs a bigger chair and table to sit at. He has light brown hair and comes from Alsace originally. And in case you think that I am just a disembodied voice, I have dark hair with a long fringe, fair skin, am wearing a white silk blouse and pearls. Oh, and my name is Rose.

The waiter pours Bourgogne Aligoté into the goldfish-bowl glasses. I love the way the wine swirls round the sides, pale gold and glistening. Leblanc tastes it and approves Richard's choice. Our first courses arrive. They are all good. The Great Architect relaxes. The evening he has created is working out. I feel something nudging against my knee. The table is obviously too small for Bruno. I move my left leg slightly to give him more space. A few minutes later, there it is again, the sensation of gaberdine brushing against my knee. I look at him. He is listening to Leblanc holding forth, his right hand loosely encircling the stem of his glass. The pressure increases. I can feel, almost hear, the rasp of trouser leg against nylon. He glances at me, a quick look, just the whites of his eyes like a colt about to nip. The knee rests against mine for a moment as if giving me time to move away. Then the nudging begins again, an up-and-down movement. There is no mistaking it. Bruno is playing kneesy with the non-threatening wife.

It takes a moment to adjust – after all, I have been invisible for some little while. I feel both amused and incensed. Bruno is bored and taking advantage of this safe situation. Well, two can play at that. I slip off my left shoe and run the sole of my stockinged foot along the calf of his leg. It feels rounded, warm through the trousers, plenty of substance, well muscled as they say in historical novels about Renaissance men in tights. I move my foot slowly up his well-muscled calf. His hand tightens around the stem of his glass. He is smiling, Leblanc has just cracked a joke. He glances at me again, a look of speculation in his eyes. The English Rose has done something unexpected.

The main courses have now arrived together with masses of vegetable dishes. Bruno turns his attention to the food and I slip my foot back into my shoe. The waiter pours Bordeaux into more glasses, velvety dark magenta. I take several swigs. It was nice, that little adventure under the table and I had surprised him. I have chosen the main course well, too. I'm having sweetbreads meunièred with capers, and long-leaved spinach, limp and lukewarm, stewed in oil and dressed in lemon juice. Everyone likes what they have chosen. We are a contented crew. I finish my plate, Bruno has finished his.

But now there is something warm resting on my knee, and it can only be Bruno's hand. I can feel the heat of it against my skin. The fingers tighten their grip and give the knee a squeeze. The hand slides along the skin and is now resting, relaxed and heavy, on my thigh. The conversation is continuing smoothly above the table. I have just made a witty contribution which Leblanc acknowledges though Richard continues unhearingly on his previous track. The fingers are beginning to move downwards to my inner thigh. Bruno must be mad. Any minute they are going to notice the disappearance of his hand and the slight movement of his arm against the cloth. I cross my legs abruptly, jolting the table, and Richard says, 'Do be careful, Rose, you nearly had everything over.'

Bruno turns an innocent smile on me. His teeth are beautiful. Richard says, 'Will you excuse me?' heaves himself to his feet and goes off to the Gents. Bruno leans towards me, we have earlier been talking about the Toulouse-Lautrec exhibition, and says, 'Rose, will you have lunch with me tomorrow and then show me the Toulouse-Lautrec exhibition?'

'You already have a lunch engagement,' says Leblanc, looking annoyed.

'Then just the afternoon,' says Bruno.

'Late afternoon. I shan't be able to leave work until four.'

'*Cinq à sept*,' murmurs Leblanc. Richard returns to the table, everyone thanks each other for a wonderful evening, and we depart into the night. I am feeling visible, again.

The next morning I say to Richard at the breakfast table after he has drunk his coffee, 'I may be working a bit late this evening.'

'That's all right. I'm not going to be back until around eleven, anyway,' says Richard through his newspaper.

'Oh, where are you going?'

Richard lowers his paper and looks at me with irritation. 'If I've told you once, I've told you a thousand times. I'm not going to keep repeating myself.'

That's one of the drawbacks about switching off when your husband is talking. You miss the occasional useful bit of information. I should have liked to have known where he will be, but at least he won't be at home wondering where I am. And I might be back early, soon after the gallery closes in fact. That might be all that happens. At least it will be worth seeing the Toulouse-Lautrec exhibition again.

It is a warm afternoon. Bruno is wearing one of those loose unstructured linen suits and an open-necked shirt. He takes off the jacket as we wander through the exhibition and hangs it from one shoulder, using his finger as a hook. The Lautrec women are exposed to our eyes, as they were exposed to the artist's unrelenting gaze. The downturned, disgusted mouth of *Fille à la Fourrure*, the bold stare of *La Femme au Boa Noir*, *La Goulue* imperious in a haze of alcohol, supported by two women like prison warders as she makes her entrance. We pause for some time at the *Salon of the Rue des Moulins*. It is obviously a quiet time of the evening for them. A desultory air hangs over the salon. The women leaning back on the banquettes gaze vacantly into the middle distance. All except one who is sitting up very straight, wearing a high-necked robe and looking out of the picture with a face on which are etched years of unhappiness and abuse. It seems almost rude to stare at her misery.

Bruno looks at her and then at me. 'You looked as miserable as that when I first met you last night.'

'I didn't!' I protest. 'We'd merely had a little tiff on the way to the restaurant.'

'When do you have to be home?' he asks.

'Richard is out until eleven.'

'So let's have a drink and then we can go on to dinner.' Bruno's arm is round my waist, he is leading me from the exhibition. I allow myself to be led. In the taxi he kisses me on the mouth, and holds my hand for the rest of the journey.

The warmth of the kiss lingers like a mark visible to all as we arrive at his hotel. It is converted from two large early Victorian houses off Ladbroke Grove and designed to make you feel as if you are a guest at someone's gracious town residence. I wander into the sitting-room while Bruno is getting his keys. It is decorated in yellow and white stripes, with antique mirrors and family portraits. Open french windows overlook a small garden. I am sure that Bruno has stayed here before.

But what is this? A constraint has fallen on us, as we sip our early evening drink, a glass of champagne in the yellow and white surroundings. We have become formal, we are

[17]

talking about the exhibition, about Bruno's work, and before long, I know it, Richard's name will come into the conversation and the evening will be ruined. The trouble is that none of my psycho-babble books help with the practicality of getting from A to B. The transition from sitting fully clothed talking over a glass of wine to being in the horizontal completely naked with someone you don't know very well is too extreme to contemplate.

My nervousness has transferred to Bruno. We have nearly two hours before we can decently go out to dinner, and I can see a miasma of thoughts behind his eyes. They have dark shadows under them, and I can hear an excuse being framed in his mind on the grounds of tiredness. We are running out of conversation, Richard's name is going to come up any moment, and then we will spend the next hour talking about people and things in whom we are not the least interested, just to avoid the speaking silence. It is obvious we have both chickened out, and it would be best to pretend that we had only wanted to see the Toulouse-Lautrec exhibition, after all. I shall make my excuses and leave.

'What are you thinking, Rose?' asks Bruno suddenly.

This is a conversation-stopper, all right. I am thinking about whether I have any food in the fridge at home. Caught on the hop, I say, as if reading Lesson 5 in an EFL textbook, 'Do you have a nice room in this hotel?'

'Come and see,' says Bruno.

It's as simple as that. I realise now that I had thrown him by sitting down in the public reception room while he was collecting the keys. I get up from the armchair. My legs feel stiff and cold. Bruno puts his hand out as if he senses I am about to stumble.

'You can help me choose a tie for dinner,' he says kindly, as if to a child or old aunt. I avoid looking at the young woman on the front desk as we walk to the lift. In its enforced proximity a cold feeling seeps through my body. I actively don't want to go to bed with this man. I don't actually like him very much any more. All he has to recommend him are a pair of well-muscled legs. The lift stops on the second floor and we walk down the corridor lined with numbered doors to Bruno's room. He turns the key in the lock, opens the door and shows me in. He closes it gently behind me, then as I stand looking round the room, puts his hands on my shoulders and draws me towards him. His mouth is on mine, his hand slides down my back, our bodies find their natural empathy and the blood is coursing through my veins. He draws back, and says, 'You do still want me, don't you?'

Oh yes, I say, and now at last we can stop hedging and look each other in the eyes again. We are both laughing with relief. His hand slides down past my buttock and under my dress.

But it is still not all right, for we are in a hotel, and two people have stopped outside our door. They are having a conversation that comes straight through the panels as if they are in the room beside us. They don't worry Bruno as his hand reaches my knickers, but they worry me.

I detach myself from him and move to the armchair by the window.

'What's wrong?' asks Bruno.

'People outside. If we can hear them, they can hear us.'

Bruno defers to my sensibilities. The lady is still jumpy. He opens the door of the small fridge built into the wall cupboard, and takes out a bottle of champagne and a bag of cashew nuts. He pours the champagne, we clink glasses and he sits on the carpet by my feet, one arm draped over my knee. The room is pretty, someone has taken a great deal of trouble with this hotel. It is all blue and white, like being

[19]

in a Delft plate. There is a patchwork quilt in a mass of different blue and white materials. The curtains match the wallpaper. It is very pretty, but small. The double bed with its white-painted wrought-iron bedstead is too close to the door.

The talking people have gone away. Bruno's hand strokes my thigh. He kneels in front of me, drawing me towards him. He kisses me and I feel his half-open mouth softly flutter over my face but I can't concentrate on him. I tell him I must go to the bathroom. As I am sitting on the lavatory I hear a cough near my ear. Someone is using the bathroom next door. There is a metallic sound as an object is dropped on the tiled floor and an audible exclamation, in a male voice, of 'Shit!' This hotel may be pretty but it has no sound insulation. Back in the bedroom I can hear through the wall the male voice talking on the phone. There is a thump overhead. Someone upstairs has either leapt out of bed or fallen over. Bruno is stroking my hair soothingly as I sit on the edge of the bed only yards from the man on the phone. I say, 'This is like being in the middle of Paddington Station.'

Bruno reaches for the knobs of the radio. There is a blast of pop music, a voice giving news of jams on the M25, and finally, a calm Radio 3 announcer promising us an evening concert called 'Mainly Baroque'. Thank heaven for that. It could have been Birtwistle. Bruno is kissing my face and neck, his hand encircling one breast. He is calling me his *petit lapin*, his *biche*. I look down at his head, now nuzzling into my breasts. He has light brown hair that smells freshly shampooed. He really is very sweet, eager yet patient. But my enthusiasm is ebbing once more, as I begin to wonder about a necessity that I had never considered before in my safe married life, I think about condoms. At what point should one ask? I have a feeling I have left it too late. When was the right time? When we were drinking champagne? At the bedroom door? They never tell you that in the Aids ads.

It's too late to retreat, in any case, for Bruno has now taken off his trousers, and there is no way you can ask a man to put them on again without irreparably injuring his dignity. He is sliding my dress off my shoulders. I say, and my voice sounds strained, 'I'm worried. We have to be careful, Bruno, I mean, could you use one of those, you know, please?'

He raises his head from my stomach. 'Don't worry, *ma petite*. I never leave home without them.'

He opens the bedside drawer and takes out a foil-wrapped object the size of a stick of chewing gum.

'You see?' he says, tearing the foil with his teeth. 'We will be perfectly safe. You must trust me, Rose, and stop thinking about all these outside things. There is only you and me here. Nothing else in the world matters.'

And then we are both lying naked in bed together. His body is warm, loving, muscular. I can feel the muscles through his skin, curving into the hollow of his spine. And he is so infinitely tender, murmuring endearments into my ear, his hands roving my body. Something is happening to me, I am overwhelmed by love. And then as that most potent muscle of all slides into me, I can hear my voice, low at first and then rising in volume and pitch, above the sound of Dido's lament. Remember me, remember me . . . My voice is out of control, there is no way I can lower it, for it has taken me over. Bruno is calling me his angel, and then no words, only gasping and moaning, and finally a shuddering cry from his depths. He raises his head, stares dizzily at me, gives a blissful smile, then falls forward on to my body like a log. I kiss his neck and shoulders again and again, loving every part of him, as I lie under him, our skin

[21]

clinging damply together with sweat. 'I love you,' I whisper. Bruno lies slumped over me and begins to snore.

I like feeling his weight on me, and I lie there listening to the music. Bruno's snoring has softened into the even breathing of one who is fast asleep. My breasts are flattened, but I don't want to disturb him. I listen to the final lyrical strings of the Mozart D Minor, a sublime mixture of the heavenly and the worldly which reflects my mood. The sun, low in the sky, sends squares of light through the window panes. The room is a peaceful haven, the only sounds now are Bruno's breathing and the music. Our various neighbours have gone off to dinner and we have the hotel to ourselves.

The Radio 3 announcer is on again to tell us what is next. It's something called 'My Point of View' for which he has gathered a clique of professional chatterers. And then the media chairman is introducing them, and I hear the voice of my husband loud and clear in our room. I try to reach for the knob but I am trapped under the weight of Bruno. My husband is beginning to expand on his special topic, the relationship of architecture and behaviour. I know it already, but this time I am forced to listen to every word as his voice cuts through the silence of the room, and through the interruptions of the other chatterers. On and on he goes, his favourite *bons mots* tumbling over each other . . . and now at last I remember him saying a week ago, that he hoped I would at least listen to his first radio broadcast. I am listening all right, as I lie there, crucified to the bed by my lover, I have no choice but to listen to the voice of my controlling husband as he talks on and on, invading my sanctum, permeating every atom of my being. The Great Architect sees all. And underneath the assured and measured tones I can hear, detectable only to me, a tremulous pride at being there on the radio, being listened to. When Bruno wakes he is surprised to find me in tears.

BURNING

Robert Edric

The first thing Oliver James noticed about the woman who was to become his first wife was the colour of her fingernails. They were the precise colour of acorns, and because of how well manicured she kept them, this was also precisely what they resembled, right down to their curved ends, their polished striations, and the pale crescents of her cuticles where the seeds sat in their cups.

He was introduced to her by a mutual friend, and the first thing Oliver James said to her was that her fingernails looked like acorns. She laughed at this and then she studied them, holding them together and closer to her face, fanning them and then turning them into her palm to inspect them against the smoother skin there. He knew by the way she allowed herself to be slowly persuaded to agree with him that she would also agree to see him again. The motion of turning her hand, of looking at the back of it and then at the soft palm, and then of folding in her fingers, had beckoned him towards her, had said to him that there was nothing about this woman that might not yet be revealed to him given time. It was as though he had exposed and then immediately understood the most intimate and dangerous of her secrets.

They spent the evening together amid a crowd of thirty or forty others, and four days later, during their second encounter, and after a meal at a restaurant on Brompton Road, they slept together.

They were married, and during the whole of their seven years together, and the sixteen years since, Oliver never forgot how the first of their fragile bonds had been struck.

The acorn-coloured nail varnish became their private code. They would be out together in public and she would take off her gloves, or find some other reason to pass her hand close across her face, and he would see the colour – perhaps on all ten nails, perhaps only on one as she entered more fully into the spirit of their signalling – and he would know immediately everything she was thinking, everything she might later make or allow to happen between them. It was the happiest time of his life.

When they separated, moving quickly apart through the cooling ashes of their fire, he looked in every drawer and cabinet of the house she was leaving to make sure that none of the acorn-coloured varnish remained.

On occasion she had painted her toenails and then slipped off one of her shoes so that he might see. On occasion she would undress or he would undress her and he would find a single small perfect circle of the colour no larger than a pea painted on her thigh or upper arm.

A month after they were married she discovered that the colour was about to be discontinued by the manufacturers, it was no longer popular, and she spent an afternoon buying up the varnish wherever she could find it, until at the end of the day she was able to sit down at her dressing-table and line up three dozen of the small tear-shaped bottles. She dare not even begin to calculate how much those thirty-six bottles held.

Afterwards, when she threw twenty of them away un-opened, and the rest were only half used, she understood how fully and easily and willingly she had entered into this self-deception, and she closed off forever that part of her life into which she had always allowed certain strangers easy access.

Oliver himself felt something similar. An edge was lost,

and for every one that went something else less well defined took its place. Excitement became thrill, and danger was reduced to chance. He made excuses, for himself and for them both, but they were the common and worthless excuses of people saying they were growing older and that the times were changing around them.

All this was long ago, sixteen years, almost seventeen, before his disillusionment and then resurrection became complete, and long before he knew that he had poured fully into the mould of his first life, had been exposed to the air and had then started to exfoliate, like a granite boulder returning to the individual grains of purer mineral it might once have been.

They entered into the machinery of their separation and kicked the last of the cold ashes from their feet. Lawyers recommended that for the sake of the machinery itself they try and remain as amicable as possible until it no longer mattered. He remembered holding out his hand to her in the presence of these men and saying, 'Friends?' and she holding out hers, gloved, and saying, 'Amicable.' The points of arrival and departure had seldom been so precisely defined.

There had been no children. Or, rather, there had been two conceived, each efficiently terminated within ten days of them making their existence known, both within the same year, the two decisions being therefore the consequence of a single judgement. That they had both been his children, Oliver was in no doubt. Infidelity had never been a problem. There had been other women and other men, but neither had allowed these to have any direct bearing on the otherwise wholly controlled and contained arrangement their marriage had quickly become.

*

On the first occasion he had gone with her to the hospital, had sat and waited with her until she was called and shown, briefly, to a bed, and had then waited for her to be brought back to it and for her to come round. He knew then, by her first glance at him, and by the flicker of recognition that crossed her eyes, that she had already started to hate him. She asked him how long he had been waiting and he said it didn't matter, but she insisted on being told. When she had recovered sufficient strength she called and asked a passing nurse how long it would be before she could leave. He knew by the way she kept forming her hands into fists and then punching them into the slack sheets between her legs that she did not want him near her, that his concern and predictability tore holes in her patience. She could no longer bear to be with him, knowing exactly what he was thinking, and how he would say it, the words and the gestures, his mannerisms and laughter.

He waited for her frustration to subside.

While he had been sitting alone he had planned a holiday for them. He told her and she laughed at him. For when all this is over? she said. Something to look forward to? He had shaken his head.

The next time he tried to speak she shouted at the top of her voice for him to shut up, picked up the magazine he had laid beside her, tore off its cover, screwed it into a ball and threw it at him. It hit his chest, fell into his lap and then on to the floor. Women in nearby beds turned to look at them. He wanted to tell them what had happened. When he next looked up at her she was studying his face. She said, 'That's that,' and he thought the same and said it back to her, wishing for the first time since he had known her that there still existed some small part of his old self that she hadn't long since taken and tested and given back to him, and that he might yet say or do or feel something she would never understand.

With his second wife it was a photograph that had been taken of the two of them together at their first meeting.

He could remember neither the occasion nor the photographer, but in the picture he is sitting on the left and leaning away from her, laughing, his right hand raised as though to protect himself from a friendly blow. Beside him she is rising from the seat, her neck craned, her chin up, her mouth open, her eyes closed. She holds out both her arms as though to steady herself. As a girl she had perfected the trick of flicking up peanuts and other small sweets and then catching them in her mouth, barely moving from where she sat or stood. This is what she had been caught doing, and the picture betrays the extent of her movement, of her preparation for the magical moment when the peanut falls into her mouth.

He remembered she had once almost choked and he had patted her back until he was thumping her and the peanut had finally been ejected. Even drunk she would catch the nut nine times out of ten.

He had the photograph in his credit card wallet, having cut it down to size until it fitted, until her body and arms were lost and her closed eyes and open mouth looked obscene.

He had intended getting rid of the picture, just as he had discarded everything else of her, but found himself unable to take it out and burn it. There had been no mistaking or confusing his feelings for the woman by the time they separated, but the photograph remained, and despite their total rejection of each other, he could still look at the picture with some affection and see only the trick, and somewhere amid the flesh tones of her face and features the invisible falling nut.

After the second divorce, a colleague laughingly accused him of misogyny, perhaps because he'd confused this with misogamy. Oliver considered this for a moment and then denied the accusation. Later, the man repeated the charge, the condemnation turned into a joke, a compliment almost. Oliver approached the man along a laughing gauntlet, said, 'I don't think so,' to his face and then pushed him in his chest, catching him unawares and causing him to fall backwards. Oliver then resisted the urge to kick him where he lay, but stood over him long enough for the man to understand that this was still an option. Everyone who had a moment ago been laughing fell silent and watched him turn and walk slowly away.

From that moment on he felt doomed. He left the office in which he was working, and then the building, got into his car in the underground car-park, drove out into the sunlight and then spent the rest of the day driving along motorways, not entirely certain where he wanted to go. He had always felt comforted by driving, even when there were no specific problems or anxieties to be smoothed away. He had once felt the same about swimming, particularly in the sea, where he could imagine himself adrift and powerless, his arms and legs and lungs beyond the control of his brain.

He left one job and took another, then another. He moved forward and then he moved sideways. He became subordinate to men over whom he had once exercised control. He started working with a man five years his junior who left his own wife just as Oliver was getting to know him, and who, in the space of a month, managed to turn himself into what seemed to Oliver to be a completely different person entirely, almost as though, pupa-like, he had been waiting for the excuse or stimulus to make the change. It also occurred to Oliver that this man had known everything about the new man he was about to become long before this metamorphosis took place, and that he had deliberately kept this new self hidden, becoming, in a sense, his own surprise, stepping out of one skin and one life and appearing fully formed in another.

It was an impossible trick, but one Oliver himself was determined to attempt.

He recalled what his first wife used to say about how it was a great shame that people seldom became the people they set out to be. Knowing about this man five years his junior would have pleased her. All things were possible, the action seemed to say, but in reality it created a test against which only total success or failure might be measured.

A month after his transformation, the man was promoted and left town. Later, Oliver heard that he had remarried. Predictably, he had already been having an affair with a younger woman, and so in Oliver's eyes, the shine of his disappearing act was dulled.

He had afterwards seen a photograph of the man with his new bride, and just by looking at them together, he knew that whatever the man wanted he would get. Some people went through their lives on straight, undiverted courses, whereas others put up their sails of whim and fashion and waited for every wind. All this had been pointed out to Oliver when he was a boy by his father, but it was only when he saw the man change that he began to believe it and to make the distinction between the two types. The woman in the picture was holding his hand in both hers, and looking up at him in a way which suggested to Oliver that she too shared his secret of change, and was perhaps herself not the woman she had been a year ago.

He once returned to the house in which he had spent his first married life. Fourteen years had passed, and he was living nearby and saw that the house was up for sale. He arranged with the estate agent to view it, asking for a time on Saturday afternoon when he would not be rushed, and because, inexplicably at that distance, he remembered Saturday afternoons as being the time when he and his wife had been at their most content in the house. They would often draw the curtains and make love on the sofa or floor with the sounds of all their neighbours and the traffic outside filtering in to them – the sound of handymen sawing and drilling and hammering, of gardeners mowing and trimming, of children playing in pools and on swings, of radios and televisions taken outside so that football and cricket matches might be listened to and watched in the sun.

He had gone back there and had seen how completely changed everything was. It had become one of the fixed laws of life, that given even the smallest opportunity, nothing must stay the same, that change could and should take place for its own sake alone and needed no further justification.

The house had been empty several months and he went from floor to floor, room to room, searching shelves and cupboards for anything that might have remained of them when they had been happy there. He found nothing, not even old familiar patterns or colours.

Less than a month later he saw his first wife again. She too must have been living nearby. She and a man were walking together along a crowded street, making a game of releasing their grip on each other and then reconnecting as people came between them. The man, Oliver saw, was as physically unlike himself as it was possible to be, and he wondered if this had played a part in his appeal.

It was then that his disillusionment became briefly tainted by self-pity.

He had a relationship of sorts with four women, all of whom he met professionally, and all of whom, he knew, made calculations about what they might have to gain by sharing their confidences with him. And on six occasions he visited expensive prostitutes. Before the first of these encounters he had expected to come away from the woman feeling dissatisfied and exposed, but instead he found himself fulfilled. She directed him to the second woman he met, the second to the third, and so on.

For the first time in eight years he was given a promotion which meant something to him. He moved home three times in a year, and although he lost money on the first transaction, he made much more on the other two. He bought a large converted flat overlooking the river. He bought it cheaply because such properties, although still sought after, were no longer in vogue. What they represented now was not what they had represented five years ago when the conversions had first been undertaken. A cast-iron girder ran the length of his new living-room, from which hung a pulley and a hook. He joked about it having been put there by the developers for when the flat owner became suicidal at the rising mortgage repayments. It had intrigued him to see which of his new acquaintances had believed him possible of this.

Twice a day the river ebbed and flowed outside his window, thick and grey or thick and brown, and clotted with flotsam, frequently appearing more substantial than the sculpted wharves and crumbling walls upon which it made its daily assaults. If the hook and pulley failed then he could always throw himself weighted from the small wrought-iron balcony.

He met a man in the branch office of the firm for which he worked – having himself become a praised and valuable asset – who taught him a new trick. 'Find a nice long empty stretch of motorway,' the man told him. 'Set yourself a course, close your eyes and count to five.' This idea appealed to Oliver immediately. He knew how horrified everyone else would be. What appealed to him most, even above the danger of such an act, was the irresponsibility of it. 'And after that start counting to ten and then fifteen.' The man had stood grinning, everything to lose and every-thing to gain by the revelation. 'The trick of it is to go into it at seventy and come out of it at seventy. A five-second man can go into it at sixty and come out at forty-five. Empty motorway, fifteen clear seconds of nothing ahead of you and nothing behind you and no bends to worry about. Keeping up the speed, that's the real test. Slowing down only increases the odds against you.' Despite himself, and conscious that he might have been putting the man who told him about this perfect test on his guard, Oliver asked him why he was telling *him* about it. 'Why not?' the man said immediately. 'There's no other way in the world you're ever going to find anything like that out about yourself.'

Several nights later, on a straight and empty stretch of dual carriageway, Oliver closed his eyes and counted quickly to three. He knew that it was not the test the man had been talking about, and that he had cheated and failed.

He repeated the exercise a week later, convinced that for

the ten short seconds his eyes had remained closed, so his heart had also stopped beating. He opened his eyes laughing. When the man asked him if he had started to experiment yet, Oliver said he hadn't, and he saw the look come into the man's eyes that told him it was to be the last of their confidences.

Two years later the man was badly injured in an accident, and immediately upon hearing this Oliver asked the woman who brought him the news if anyone else was involved. No, she said. The man had been fixing a receiver dish to his roof when he had slipped and fallen to the ground. Both his legs were broken, and all but one of his ribs down his right-hand side. Oliver visited him in hospital, and guessing what Oliver imagined, the man tried not to laugh but was soon gasping with pain. Close your eyes, Oliver had thought, and perhaps it will all go away.

It occurred to him then that he had become a much harder, a much crueller man than he had once been. He chose to think of it as being desensitised. He did not avoid the truth, but like everything else the truth was open to endless manipulation without any real loss.

He left the hospital and found himself laughing aloud as he threaded through the cars back to his own. Anyone watching him, he imagined, would mistake his heartlessness for relief.

A month later he met a man, a customer, who told him over dinner one evening that he was having an affair with a woman twenty years younger than himself, who was an actress, and who was currently spending most of her days dressed as a mermaid at a travelling aquarium which had set up in a tent for Easter in the park where he had taken his children. He described to Oliver his infatuation with the woman, building up detail after detail of her costume, of her long blonde wig and the way she sat on a fibreglass boulder and took the money of the people entering the exhibition. She had been dressed like this the first time they had made love, her tail being pulled off only at the last uncontrollable moment.

Oliver found himself intrigued. He asked the man which he found the most exciting – the age difference or the costume. The man had to think about this, and then he disappointed Oliver by choosing the age difference. Oliver decided to see the woman for himself.

He went to the park early on Sunday morning before the crowds had gathered and before the aquarium was open. He waited at the largest of the tents, the one advertising the sharks, for a woman fitting the man's description to appear. None came. Instead a short, plain woman with black hair appeared. She sat on a stool at the entrance to the tent and smoked three cigarettes in succession. Oliver watched her. He saw her take out her packet for the fourth and then throw it to the ground to crush it with her foot. He approached her, asked her when the exhibits were open to the public and took out his own cigarettes. He waited until she was watching him and then offered her one. They started talking and he told her he'd heard about the mermaid who sat inside. It was her, she said without enthusiasm. She looked at him suspiciously, as though he had known all along. 'A silver tail on a leotard, blonde wig, glitter over my cheeks, cockle shells on my – ' She shaped her hands. 'Cinderella job. I was the first the uniform fitted.'

He asked her if the fish were worth seeing. Only the sharks, she said. She told him about the hammerhead which kept cracking its ugly head against the glass and scaring her to death. He gave her another cigarette. She told him she smoked thirty a day but was not allowed to smoke on duty. A smoking mermaid would not have been good for business. He gave her his packet and arranged to meet her later.

For the first time in five years, he found himself looking forward to something over which he so far had so little control. His first decision was to take her away from the dull man who found only her comparative youth exciting.

He saw her that night, and for the two nights following, on the last of which she appeared with a small yellow bruise on her cheek and lied to him about having fallen off her fibreglass boulder having tried to stand too quickly in her tight-fitting tail.

The next day Oliver did two things. First he started a rumour that the man who had hit her was unreliable and a thief and ought not to be trusted; and second he went to see the woman dressed in her mermaid outfit.

She was exactly as he imagined she would be, and because of this he was disappointed. He could understand the appeal of her to someone who had not seen beneath the silver scales and the wig and the shells, but he was able to look straight through the costume and see her only as he had seen her so far.

The massive grey tent let in little natural light and the tank at its centre was illuminated by an arrangement of spotlights. The pale undersides of the sharks showed occasionally through the gloom as they came close to the glass and then flicked away from it at the last moment, their eyes and teeth glimpsed only for an instant. The water in the tank was dark green and opaque and filled with coarse sediment in suspension. Most of the people gathered around it were disappointed by what little they could see, and only the youngest children appeared genuinely enthusiastic at the sudden glimpses. The creatures inside moved effortlessly to and fro, like half-remembered shapes in a nightmare. Men waited with cameras, their flashes bursting against the glass.

It was difficult for Oliver to talk to the woman. Customers were still coming in. Others complained to her on their way out and she feigned helpless sympathy until they were gone. She flicked her tail at their backs. He was about to speak to her when they were finally alone, but she pointed over his shoulder and said, 'Quick, the hammerhead.' He turned to see the tube-shaped head collide with the glass, and never in his life had he seen anything so ugly, and so threatening in its ugliness, so close. He waited for the creature to reappear, but it never came. Beside the tank a small girl started crying, and her father tried unsuccessfully to calm her. Eventually the man picked her up and carried her outside, glancing angrily at Oliver and the woman as he went.

Oliver followed him out several minutes later. He would not see her again, and she understood this as well as he did. He kept the ticket she had given him, but that was all.

Outside he was joined by a park attendant, a man who looked ten years beyond retirement age, and who approached Oliver and asked him if he had ever heard of anything so ridiculous as a travelling aquarium or women dressed as mermaids. Oliver agreed with him. The man wiped his face with a cloth. It was unseasonably warm, and with the forecast of a possible thunderstorm later in the day. The man said the storm was definitely coming, and that it would be here sooner than anyone expected. The confidence of this prediction amused Oliver and he asked the man how he knew. But the old man shook his head and would not say. Oliver asked him again, and the man moved away from him, looking up into the darkening sky as though he were already waiting for the first vivid crack of lightning to suddenly appear and prove him right.

THE WHITE
SOFA

Keto von Waberer

translated by Peter Filkins

Frau Reinsbeck knew immediately that it was the Devil. He sat on the white sofa in front of the television and laughed, his bony knees propped up like locust legs, his naked skin glowing a greenish white. On the screen fish swam back and forth, their thick lips snapping open and shut as they passed through the swaying seaweed.

Through the half-opened door Frau Reinsbeck took it all in. The key in her hand, she stood in the hallway, a grocery bag pressed to her chest. A garlic bulb tickled her chin.

Frau Reinsbeck smiled as she noticed that he had no horns or cleft foot. She was not a good Christian, but it surprised her that the Devil, of all people, was sitting on her sofa. He must seek out those he thinks he can impress. Meanwhile she carried the groceries into the kitchen, arranged the vegetables in a basket on top of the refrigerator, placed the milk and cheese on the shelf inside, then pulled off the black coat with the fur collar and ran her fingers through her hair. In the living room she could hear him laughing. The sound was exaggerated and reminded her of something she might hear at the zoo. Most likely he had heard her come in.

With a quick, firm step she walked down the hall and stood at the door.

A fish nibbled at a mossy stone and fanned its translucent fins, its gills opening and closing. There was nothing funny about it.

Selected from 'Der Schattenfreund,' by Keto von Waberer © 1988 Verlag Kiepenheuer & Witsch, Koln.

The Devil looked up at her with the idiotic grimace of someone who had been laughing uncontrollably and could not stop but who was trying to get a hold of himself. His pale hair sat curled on top of his head like dirty foam. The forehead, much too high, was crowned with quivering fur; his eyes were moist.

Frau Reinsbeck stood there in high heels with her arms crossed and cleared her throat.

With his arms he made slow, elegant movements as in 'Kung Fu' on television, then crossed his hands and pointed at her with raised middle fingers, and with a low curving motion indicated the spot next to him on the sofa.

'Come, Lizzie,' he said, his voice bright and trembling with laughter. No one had called her Lizzie since her childhood.

As he unzipped her dress, she thought about the ugly bump on the nape of her neck. She had often observed it from the side while looking in the mirror. A hump like that of a brown bear. Sitting at the typewriter had caused it, bowing down before the card file and lowering her head whenever Herr Gallwitz –

'Impotent!' he said, interrupting her thoughts. His voice was firm.

He kissed the little peak of flesh that pressed out of a hole in her stocking that had been there since morning at the top of her thigh. She too had noticed it but had kept the stockings on anyway.

Seen from above, his hair now seemed as transparent as cellophane noodles. He wore light-coloured underwear that was baggy and not very clean.

'Who is impotent?'

'Gallwitz.'

Frau Reinsbeck laughed, for she had often wished it on him.

She noticed that he had taken the bottle of cognac out of the sideboard. It stood next to his naked foot. His toenails were filthy.

In the green underwater light Frau Reinsbeck watched tiny glittering fish flit across the screen. Her breasts green, and below them the slimy raised mound of her belly. His hand disappeared, and now the fish swam towards her and over her, passing through her open thighs, pecking at her, sucking, nibbling with their mouths. His hand crawled like a slow crab, excited and intent, over the hill of her breast.

'Look, Lizzie.'

She had already noticed the raised tent of his lap towards which he now pulled her hand. It glowed like phosphorous, casting eerie shadows, something fidgeting within as she grasped it firmly and with pleasure.

He lifted her on to his lap very lightly and entered her smoothly. Feeling an itch, a little pain, a slippery fish, then something like warm metal, Frau Reinsbeck giggled.

Halos of sand drifted above a starfish that hardly moved.

Wrapped in the sound of flesh and murmurs, Frau Reinsbeck rocked from wave to wave. On and on it went, her eyes half closed.

Letters marched across the screen like silver ants.

As a woman in a blue flowered dress stared out at them with eyes opened wide and went on and on, mouthing mute words with glossy lips, Frau Reinsbeck gasped.

The Devil reeked of burnt celluloid; his teeth were sharp. He bit into her shoulder, her throat.

'What do I have to give you?' whispered Frau Reinsbeck. 'My soul?' A sob of laughter escaped through her nose.

He rolled his eyes, and because Frau Reinsbeck felt she could not hold his gaze any longer, she closed her own.

*

She had not expected that he would move in; he never announced his arrival, and one could hardly give him the trash to take out when he left. He was suddenly there and suddenly gone. Exactly when she never knew precisely, though he always came at night. On some nights he was so transparent and ephemeral that Frau Reinsbeck could reach right through him as she straightened things up.

'Felt terrible today,' he would say. His hair circled his face like muddy light. Frau Reinsbeck kept the apartment as warm as a terrarium. She walked around naked and bent down to gather up plates and glasses that lay about between the furniture. He ate and ate, and she lugged home heavy grocery sacks of chipped beef and blood sausages, pickled and jellied meats, and no vegetables.

At the office no one noticed how she kept to herself. Herr Gallwitz remained standing at the door whenever he gave her dictation. Fräulein Leeb turned up her nose whenever she saw Frau Reinsbeck squeezing her hips between the photocopier and the file cabinet with a groan. He, on the other hand, weighed her breast in his hand like a fruit vendor, gripped her stomach like a warm loaf of bread.

'What does Hell look like?' They sat on the white sofa watching the weather report. Frau Reinsbeck spoke the word *Hell* as if referring to a spa, uttering it coyly in order to let him know that she didn't believe in Hell. She giggled.

He yawned and stretched his arms, his joints snapping. 'There is no Hell,' he said and placed an olive in Frau Reinsbeck's navel.

'Where do you live?' asked Frau Reinsbeck quickly.

'In a cramped little room full of furniture, pink gardenias, and faded persian carpets.' He looked at her. 'Two windows – not very clean.' He reached up to touch her eyes, causing her to suddenly blink. 'Or in a red room,' he laughed. 'With an animal hide for a door.'

There was no talking with him.

'You have to knock before you enter.'

He knocked.

There was no talking with him.

On some days Frau Reinsbeck didn't go to work. She called in, pinching her nose as she spoke. She stayed in bed the entire day and later got up to lie down on the white sofa in front of the television. She chatted with the announcer, praising his poise and erudition. She got caught up in debates and pounded her hand on the table in order to drive her point home. Sometimes, out of the side of her eye, she saw strange animals lurking between the furniture. The carpet fringe lifted up and wriggled. Shadows scurried back and forth beneath the table. But he didn't come, didn't show up, and she went to bed with a book about the Prince of Darkness. Whoever had written it didn't know what he was talking about.

Frau Reinsbeck sometimes found his humour a bit hard to take. The trick that involved the disappearing fish finger, or the lewd arrangement of lettuce leaves around a piece of meat on a bed of white rice. She let him have his fun. Then came the recorded sounds. Were they music? Human voices could be heard howling like hyenas or trilling like tree frogs between drumbeats and clock chimes. Sweet, soft flute tones, sultry and disturbing. One after another, waves of goose bumps travelled over Frau Reinsbeck.

'It's played on bones.' Frau Reinsbeck didn't ask what kind of bones.

Lipsticks appeared overnight like mushrooms in front of the bathroom mirror. Cyclamen red, shades of purple, hot pink. And the yellow dress. Just where had it come from and for whom was it meant? He looked like a dragonfly larva when he wore it, emerging from his pupa with a mass of twitching legs. In comparison Frau Reinsbeck looked like a plump Chinese pincushion, he said, and for hours afterward they would play the sewing game.

Sometimes his jokes were tasteless. He would sit on the sofa dressed in the blue fireman's uniform of her late husband, his head wrapped in a bandage, or beat time to the rapid gunfire of a western, or hang Fräulein Leeb up naked by her heels in the bathroom. Her beautifully manicured red nails swayed back and forth above the shag rug in front of the tub.

Once, just as Frau Reinsbeck was about to climax beneath him on the white sofa, managing to catch a fleeting glimpse of a Japanese dance troupe that was performing on the third channel, he imitated the mating call of the short-tailed oriole in her father's voice. When she was a child, Frau Reinsbeck's father had been an avid hunter and bird caller. For days after this little farce, Frau Reinsbeck felt bad whenever she thought of the old man, who now lived in a trailer and occasionally sent her postcards of campgrounds in Yugoslavia and Greece.

Frau Reinsbeck soon realized that she could not be involved with the Devil without paying a price. On the subway men made silent but suggestive signs towards her; garbage trucks

roared outside her window as early as six; and at the movies
an old man, who had appeared nearly blind and slumped
over while dozing in the seat next to her, suddenly leaned
against her as she was reaching into her purse, a damp little
umbrella held erect in his hand. Worst of all were the dogs
that occasionally chased the milk truck, stopping to shove
their cold noses underneath her dress and up her legs. If it
was him they could smell on her, then it was also him that
Fräulein Leeb could smell when, with the excuse of needing
a couple of paper clips from her desk, she bent over her and
in a hoarse voice whispered 'What's that perfume?' Nonetheless, the attention pleased her.

And on Thursday evenings Frau Reinsbeck cleaned up at
bridge, beating the other ladies effortlessly and with no
qualms. 'You're playing devilishly well, Elizabeth,' said the
ladies with nodding heads, 'but you've put on weight, and
don't you think the blood-red lipstick is a little much?' She
lost the next hand and would have gone home to have a
cognac, thus pleasing her pale-skinned lover, but mistrust
of him and his ideas kept her where she was.

She cancelled her mother's visit. It wasn't easy to do, for
as she spoke into the phone with a nasal quality that had
come from too much overtime and a bout with the flu, she
could hear him whistling and sizzling away in the kitchen.
As a result, she didn't feel right for the rest of the evening,
and he vanished with a 'Ciao, mama,' right before the
detective movie started. He left behind him a haze of garlic.

Sometimes she was caught by an inexplicable sense of
fear at the threshold of her apartment. Church hymns and
organ music surged through her head, visions of parch-
ments signed with blood, and the winged and violet-haired
shapes of spirits she remembered observing on church walls
in Italy on her honeymoon – grinning faces that bent over
screaming women, trying to drag them away by the hair,

pitiless and full of zeal, as if harvesting a crop that was rightfully and legally theirs.

Later she would touch the bald spots on his head with a slight feeling of trepidation, and he would look at her with narrowed eyes and grin.

'If one horn isn't enough for you, I'll sprout two more above,' he said and bucked at her side like a ram.

'Are we doing something evil?' asked Frau Reinsbeck, trembling.

'Of course we are, Lizzie,' he said, imitating her father exactly. 'My little silken lamb.'

At the Gallwitz & Schellenberger Christmas party, Frau Reinsbeck wore the yellow dress. In the spirit of the season, Herr Gallwitz, beaming, was decked out in a Norwegian sweater. A sprig of mistletoe was stuck in the brown curls behind his ear. He danced with Frau Reinsbeck again and again, and during a tango grabbed her left breast with such fervor that she slapped his ear.

Later, when with a tentative hand he reached for a paper cup full of beer from the rows of cups lined up on the bar, she heard him mutter to the red-faced clerk, 'A real she-devil.'

Fräulein Leeb had borrowed Frau Reinsbeck's lipstick and painted her lips with patient meditation, meanwhile casting melancholy glances at Frau Reinsbeck in the mirror.

Frau Reinsbeck's mother refused to stay away any longer and came to visit for Christmas. She knitted new covers for the pillows on the sofa.

Before she arrived, Frau Reinsbeck had lain awake most nights, imagining the confrontation between her mother and her nightly guest. When she mentioned her fears to him, he laughed uncontrollably and let loose with crude and distasteful comments about her mother. Frau Reinsbeck knew she could not dictate his arrival times, but she feared that her mother's presence might effectively keep him away, and this upset her. She decided to introduce him as her boyfriend, dropping hints to her mother on the phone, hoping that, should a meeting occur, it could be dealt with easily right then and there. In an emergency, she could always give her mother a sleeping pill. By the time her mother arrived, Frau Reinsbeck was in such a state that the thought of dosing her own mother brought on relief without a trace of guilt.

Of course he was nowhere to be seen as, night after night, her mother sat on the white sofa, playing solitaire and asking if there was anything on television. She liked only certain shows – talk shows, game shows, and folk music. Everything else bored her.

'Where then is your fiancé?' she asked without much interest, though with a hint of malice, for she had long given up believing her daughter capable of marrying again. Frau Reinsbeck, queasy from nightly servings of bread pudding and stewed cherries, and worn out by long motherly monologues about the uncertain quality of store-bought baked goods, the health of the corn crop, and the irresponsibility of her wayward father, gave no answer.

Instead, one day Herr Gallwitz appeared before the door with a gaudy bouquet of flowers, and Frau Reinsbeck's mother cantered about like a fluttering girl as she brewed tea in the kitchen and sang the praises of his suit, his well-groomed fingernails, and the sweet, lingering scent of his carnation soap.

[49]

Later, as Frau Reinsbeck's mother rinsed out the teapot in the kitchen, Herr Gallwitz knelt before the sofa and told Frau Reinsbeck that, after careful thought, and while acknowledging the possibility of her refusal, and despite his own feeling of foolhardiness, considering his age . . . now that he . . . He plucked the bouquet from the vase and held it to his chest.

'You want me to – ' she interjected, but she had hardly spoken when Herr Gallwitz, his eyes shifting nervously back and forth, interrupted her just in time.

'No, not that . . . no, not that, Elizabeth, if I may call you that at a time like this. I want to marry you.'

How could Frau Reinsbeck respond to that?

That night Frau Reinsbeck went to bed early and thought about her situation.

Her mother stayed up unusually late watching television, and mentioned the next morning at breakfast that she had nodded off.

'Suddenly, Lizzie, suddenly there sat a young man next to me on the sofa. I don't think he had anything on but a pair of underwear. He looked a lot like Friedhelm. I've told you about Friedhelm, haven't I? My first love. Later he became a priest.' She buttered her roll and glanced around the table.

'No sausage?' she asked. 'No gherkins?'

Frau Reinsbeck stirred a spoonful of marmalade into her coffee. Her mother had not yet finished.

'Those eyes,' she giggled. 'Bedroom eyes, we used to call them – my goodness, what a dream that was! Friedhelm never had such eyes . . . now that I think about it, the boy didn't look at all like Friedhelm. And now I – I feel so much like . . . but as an old woman, I'm ashamed to admit it.'

[50]

'And then what happened?' asked Frau Reinsbeck, her voice thick.

'Oh, you know . . .' said Frau Reinsbeck's mother. Her cheeks were flushed and she chewed on a piece of roll that was much too big, not noticing the marmalade that dribbled down her chin. 'Nothing . . . nothing . . . what do you think . . . I simply woke up.' She laughed until tears filled her eyes.

'You pig, you ass!' shrieked Frau Reinsbeck. Her mother was startled and stared back at her.

'I wasn't talking to you,' said Frau Reinsbeck.

'Child, you are so strange of late. Maybe you're going through the change.'

That afternoon Frau Reinsbeck took her to the station.

Each evening, when Frau Reinsbeck came home from the office, she expected to find him squatting on the sofa, but it was already February and the apartment lay in darkness, the television cold, whenever she stood in the hallway, at the door.

She didn't bring Herr Gallwitz to the apartment, visiting him at his place instead. At first he had a great deal of difficulty knowing just what he should offer her. The tea he brewed was too weak, and on his television the picture faded in and out and wiggled back and forth limply. Frau Reinsbeck, who feigned interest as he talked about his years as a travelling salesman, spreading a linen napkin over her naked knee and placing before her a piece of chocolate cake that he had bought specially, tried her best to give him some hint of what move to make.

[51]

But nothing good came of it. It didn't even help that when Herr Gallwitz played her his collection of old tango records, translating the text with a quavering voice, Frau Reinsbeck twirled seductively across the floor wearing only an openwork shawl. At the same time, it pleased her that Herr Gallwitz was not a bad man, and that when he took off his glasses his eyes were pale and full of innocent hope.

Finally one rainy afternoon Frau Reinsbeck accidentally discovered how to take the melancholy Herr Gallwitz in hand and help him get aroused. She told him about the games played on the white sofa. She turned the Devil into a young student and herself into a famous actress and packed the both of them between the covers of a book that she had read on vacation.

'Shame on the Devil,' whispered Herr Gallwitz, his eyes glowing in the half-darkness.

Frau Reinsbeck felt around under the blanket and found what she was seeking.

'Tomorrow you should buy a big television,' she said, but Herr Gallwitz was breathing heavily and did not hear her.

'Your mother has dyed her hair red,' her father wrote. 'She doesn't want me to visit her any more. She's happy just to watch television and eat. Still, I think she needs me. Maybe she's sick. I should be near her in this time of crisis. I want to move in with her again, because my rheumatism really bothers me, but she won't have it. Talk to her.' On the postcard was a picture of a camp in Saxony.

*

In the spring, when Frau Reinsbeck lay on the white sofa with a sore throat and low-grade fever, watching a children's show, there came over her a familiar and comfortable feeling of uneasiness, and she closed her eyes to keep it from disappearing. He was next to her, sprawled out on the pillows as usual, and she noticed between her fluttering eyelids that he was wearing black bikini briefs. She tugged at the hair on his chest, which was dark brown, brown as the tufts that stood on his head like a cockscomb, his damp curls pulled back behind his ears, his hair wiry in the light on the television.

'What's this you're wearing?' she asked in a sulky voice.

'I go with the times.'

As usual, he made no great fuss over her illness but simply took the compress from her throat and began to unbutton her nightgown. He looked to see if everything was still there for his bidding and awaiting his pleasure, knowing well the effect of his masterly hand. Frau Reinsbeck recognised it as well and followed his movements from beneath half-closed eyelids.

'Tell me how you've been,' he said, without missing a stroke of his caresses.

Frau Reinsbeck giggled. She pulled the silky underwear down over his bony knees and began to recite a poem that had come into her head. It was about a dove that, while flying, had become disoriented and came to land under a jacket, beneath a blouse and into the heart of a woman. She didn't know just why she recited it to him. He laughed, pecked at a mole, cooed, and then said that some birds certainly were stupid, and that doves especially had never impressed him.

As always, time flew, and by the time Frau Reinsbeck had regained her vision the late show was already on.

The Devil's head lay heavy upon her, its curls pressed to

her breast, making it look as if she were also covered with hair, while his snoring seemed to her particularly endearing.

For a while she watched absentmindedly as heavy-set men in suits shook each others' hands and kissed each other on the cheeks at the same time.

Still nestled against her breast, he grunted and pressed against her. Never before had he slept by her side. He must be exhausted. What had compelled him to stay? She had never noticed the creases between his nose and the corners of his mouth. And as she studied him in a somewhat motherly fashion, a little jealous, it suddenly occurred to her how much, really, he looked like Herr Gallwitz. Her head was still light with fever, and she knew that in the last few years her eyesight had weakened, especially when something impenetrable lay before her eyes.

THE CROW WHO
ANSWERED THE PHONE

Jamie O'Neill

Dido Poynings was weighing up the starlings. Saucy little madams, she decided. The sort who gravitate to the back of class, scratch heart signs on their desk tops. Faithless too: filch from their own as soon as from others. Poor sparrows hardly get a look-in. However. She drummed her fingers on her folded arms. She could deal with starlings. Dido Poynings had spent a lifetime dealing with unruly elements. She rapped sharply on the window and the starlings scattered to the far trees. The sparrows, smaller, hungrier no doubt, remained.

She believed she preferred sparrows. They sat near the front, continued their lives with neat constancy. Uninspiring name, though, you had to admit. Sparrow: meaning . . . well, sparrow. Starling sounded so much more poetic. That was the trouble with language, with society probably. Made poesy of madams and disregarded the industrious.

She had fed the birds. There was very little cleaning to do because the bulk of her furniture had not yet arrived. Delayed in Hartlepool, the man had said. It seemed an odd place for furniture to fetch up. County Durham, she believed. Shipbuilding and fishing the main industries. No doubt it wasn't called County Durham any more. Something new, metropolitan.

The village clock was striking the three-quarter hour. Perhaps she should make a pot of tea. Except her teapot was with her furniture. It was difficult to picture Crown Derby in Hartlepool. Blue-ringed mugs seemed far more likely. Am I being uppity? I'll use a tea-bag.

She was waiting for the kettle to boil when the phone rang. For a moment she felt disorientated, then she remembered the phone was in the hall. Her feet resounded on bare boards. Everywhere in the house was such a long way. She picked up the receiver. She was still unfamiliar with the number, so she just said, 'Hello.' Then, 'Hello?' But there was no reply. Just before she put the receiver down she believed she caught a whisper from the other end, a breath only. But she couldn't be certain.

MacNamara visited for sherry the next Sunday. 'Telephone calls?' he said.

'Yesterday's was the seventh.'

'And there's never a soul at the other end?'

'Never.'

MacNamara quaffed his sherry. 'Hooligans,' he pronounced. 'I warned you, Dido. They have the country terrorised. Banjaxed it is.'

He had warned her, it was true. MacNamara had played Cassandra for thirty years in the letters attached to his Christmas cards. 'More sherry?' she asked.

'I will,' he said. Then as the sherry was poured, expansively, 'Settling in, I see.'

At the drinks tray Dido wondered was he being friendly – encouraging, so to speak – or merely ironic. If he were a child, a pupil, she'd point him toward his error. 'Not settling in, child. I pour from a bottle not a decanter, into tumblers rather than tulips. Powers of deduction, child: sharp eyes sharpen wits.' But MacNamara wasn't a pupil. He was a doctor, one of her dearest friends. He addressed her that way in his letters. 'My dearest friend,' they began. 'How are you?'

She delivered the tumbler of sherry. They sat side by side on the sofa. The armchairs were in Hartlepool. 'It will take a while,' Dido said, 'before I find my feet.'

'Still,' said MacNamara. He sipped from his glass, then growled a long cough. 'Good sherry, that. A good thick broth of a job.'

He's lived in Yorkshire since his college days, thought Dido. His regular pew in the church, own corner in the pub, he's one of the county's committee men. Yet not a trace of his Irish has he dropped in all these years. Must be going to night classes. Then again, perhaps it isn't so odd. I've travelled the world, teaching. Don't suppose my accent's changed noticeably. Still crisp, professional, BBC orthodox. Received, they used to call it.

Must be nice being Irish, it occurred to her suddenly. You can be educated and successful, and still sound as if you come from somewhere.

There was no fire in the grate – the coalman hadn't delivered. Two electric fires whined in the background. Dido realised they were staring at a blank wall. The wallpaper, generally faded, was less so in places, where pictures had hung. Other people's dispositions. I'll have to re-wallpaper. The house still felt like someone else's, as if it was waiting for a buyer, under offer, so to speak, and she was the caretaker. 'Tell me,' she said, 'I was wondering: who lived here before?'

'Before you? The place has stood empty eighteen months or more.'

Damp, thought Dido.

'A single man had it then. Off-comer at that. Never a good idea. 'Tis a family home. Great big garden. Crying out for children, so it is. Young blood, that's what the village needs. Och!' He hit his temple with the mound of one hand. 'What am I saying? I didn't mean that at all. Nothing of the sort.'

She would have let it pass, but his compunction insisted.

'Sure, you're part of the village, Dido. Of course you'll

be welcome. You taught at the school here for goodness' sake. Naturally you wanted to come back.'

How very persuasive. She felt she must intervene. 'And Joyce, of course, was born here.'

'You'll have to forgive me, Dido. I hadn't forgotten. It's just . . .' He slapped his thigh a few times, unsettling the change in his pocket. He sighed. His hands gestured futility. 'I'm sorry, Dido,' he said. 'Truly.'

He had made her feel mean, visiting her troubles on these village folk. She poured no more sherry.

In the hall, waiting for his coat, he said unexpectedly. 'Don't mind about the phone calls.'

Dido stuttered. 'Well, I wasn't – '

'Mind you, Giggleswick has changed. Giggleswick? The whole country is banjaxed. On its last legs. Not the same place you left, how long is it now? Getting on. Must be twenty, twenty-five years.'

'Twenty-nine,' said Dido.

'You don't say.'

He was eyeing her queerly. Dido had the feeling he might be hesitating over a prescription. He was half-way into his coat. His arm had missed the armhole.

'*Tempus fugit*,' he said. Then, 'You know, Dido, you don't look hardly a day older.'

His little gallantry. She smiled tinily, watching his back in the hall mirror as he struggled with his coat. He was still the MacNamara of old, though his broad shoulders stooped now with time rather than awkwardness. The banter hadn't changed, that doctor's mix of bluster and blunder that came apparently with the bag. How clumsy were his hands, as though accustomed from birth to a nurse's attendance. Suddenly, she remembered that this dearest friend had never married. Oh no, she disclaimed, not on my account, certainly not. Her smile that had lingered went chill with the thought.

MacNamara looked over his shoulder embarrassed. She relaxed her frown especially for him and, confidence restored, he found the armhole.

'Don't hesitate to call,' he entrusted, 'should you need anything. Company, like.' His head nodded solicitously ' – Joyce and all.' He donned his hat. 'God rest her soul.' He was still dithering. 'And thanks for the sherry.'

Go, she urged, and finally he was gone. She bolted the door. They'd known each other since their early twenties, when she was a probationary teacher at the nearby school for girls and he was the young college doctor. Together with Joyce and Joyce's fiancé they had made a foursome. They'd corresponded down the years, but Dido believed it was at MacNamara's insistence. If she remembered correctly, he liked to collect stamps.

It came as small surprise that in a man-made world life should be cosier for men. Easier to fall, she granted, but with the corresponding advantage that success was obvious. Had a woman been Grand Artificer her life perhaps would not have changed, but the assumptions regarding it would be less doubtful. MacNamara's bachelorhood seemed to enhance his standing, made romance of his sporadic failings. Whereas for her, generations of educated girls counted as little against a home-made brat of her own. 'You've kept your maiden name, then,' the old postmistress had remarked. 'Still, not too late.'

But how absurd they were when confronted with emotions, like eager dogs in need of a pat. She had never disliked men, or rather, never abhorred them like some of her acquaintance. She believed at one time she might have loved one. Then came Joyce, of course. For a while she had worried that Joyce would fall for a man. But now the idea seemed nonsensical. How could so sparkling a mind as Joyce's have found anything but irritation in that humdrum creation called man?

There were some good walks around the village and she might take MacNamara with her for company. It tickled her the way he showed off his Latin, as though the botanical names for flowers and things were a masculine mystery. And the peculiar way they have of avoiding your eyes – Don't show me your soul, as if to say, but *anima* is the word in Latin.

The telephone calls continued. It was a nuisance more than anything else. Dido might be feeding the birds or watching them feed from the kitchen or sitting-room window and she'd have to drop whatever she was doing and chase into the hall to answer the phone. And the hall was the room she disliked most in the house because – she wasn't sure why – because the phone was there probably. Many times she promised she'd ignore its ringing, but her resolve was ultimately frustrated. She was worried it might be news from Hartlepool, though it never was. There was only silence at the other end, or at most a thin, barely audible breathing.

She was careful not to neglect her own needs. She cooked in the evening – not well, she allowed, but nutritiously. Cookery had never been her subject, although she had taken a class in domestic science for one term. That was in Uganda at the beginning of the bad times. All the teachers had to double up, and Joyce took her through the basics. No, what she really lacked were the finishing touches. A particular spice, appetising arrangement on the plate, decent plates even. A little grace, she thought at table one evening. She let her fork fall into the mash on her plate. 'Oh Joyce,' she said. For a moment she thought she would cry, but no, she didn't cry. She did the washing-up.

She had Joyce's picture beside her bed. It was in a silver frame with a dove ascending from the top and trefoils and beading along the edges. Tactually, it was interesting. Often she would hold it in her hands, rubbing a finger along the filigree. From the photograph Joyce looked out, a grin in the eyes that was knowing, impish, as though she had just played a trick on the photographer. How well she knew those eyes. She had followed them from Cape to Gulf, the stretch of a continent. On patios and terraces, across countless tables, in all weathers and hours without end. Dido had stared into those eyes. She had found peace there. She had looked where she loved. Now she gazed at a photograph. The co-ordinates of her life, dates and places, she had at her fingertips. But facts were not what she sought. And though she stared till her vision was blurred and she held the picture till her grip went white, still she felt lacking.

When they had wheeled Joyce back from the theatre, unexpectedly early, they had ushered Dido outside the waiting-room. 'So sorry,' they said, 'but there's no hope.' 'What do you mean?' 'Gangrene in the stomach. We can't operate.' 'Yes, but what do you mean?'

What they meant was that Joyce had to die. It took six hours. They took out most of the wiring and tubes and every half-hour or so they injected Valium into her veins. Her hand went cold, her breathing ebbed, less than a whisper, a mode of the air. Dido would turn to the nurse. 'Not yet,' would come the reply. It took six hours.

In the end, like the realisation of night, death was

[63]

obvious. In Joyce's eyes was the glassy reflection of a woman stooping. Her own eyes, Dido knew, reflected a corpse. She's dead, she said and left.

They gave her Joyce's headphone set, the one she listened to her operas on, some clothes and her toilet bag, then Dido went home. Their bedrooms connected with louvred doors. There was the tumble of Joyce's clothes on her chairs, on her table the cram of her perfumes, her scrapbook of recipes lay open in the galley. Everything was presented, but senselessly so, as in some ghastly mime of continuance. Dido sat on a hard-backed chair that neither had ever used. This apartment no longer felt home. It was a museum: this is how two women lived in the late twentieth century, expatriates in an oil-rich state, sharing. She went to school the next day, but she could tell they were uneasy. Her eyes kept glazing, she felt they were marbles whose central stripe showed a grey corpse stiffening. The principal drove her home. She waited there. She believed she wanted to cry, but she could summon no focus for her distress. Museums, whose business is the past, are the places in this world least haunted by it.

For the first time in years she slept in Joyce's bed. By morning the sheets smelt of Dido. She wore her nightdress, but the nurses – gratuitously – had returned it laundered. It smelt of hospital: the clean hygienic smell that contrarily marks illness, suffering, death. She tried Joyce's perfume, *Lily-of-the-valley*, but on her wrists the scent was too strong, like a cheap thing, artificial. Nothing was right. Her every pore, breath, heartbeat, every hair that dropped on the pillow marked a further severance. How the quick vanquish the dead – involuntarily, viscerally, unmercifully. Even the music Joyce liked sounded wrong: a changed orchestra, a brash young conductor. She needed to hold something, cling something to her. But the evaporation of

Joyce was inexorable, like rain from the desert. Soon there would be nothing at all, just sand like the sand in an hour-glass that has slipped through time.

She accompanied the coffin back to England. Joyce's people were at the terminal. All lined up, thought Dido, like greeters. 'Pleased . . . sorry . . . meet again . . . trying circumstances . . .' Shake hands, eyes elsewhere, home to England, land of discretion. Then to the store marked 'Special Consignments' where they waited for the box. Silence, edged in smiles. But their whirlwind assumption of 'the arrangements' when the box slid into view, hissed their vituperation.

How could you let this happen? She was our daughter. Call yourself a friend? Why didn't you look after her? Get your hands away, you can't be trusted. Who are you, anyway? We're blood and you're water, vapid thinly stuff, under the bridge.

Dido went to the car-hire and arranged her own way north.

Joyce's father had retired from Giggleswick, where he had been rector, and now lived in a dormitory town the other side of the Dales. The trees in the gardens looked flimsy and shadeless, the borders everywhere were munici-pally neat – like an expatriate colony, thought Dido. How Joyce would mock. She booked into a guest house.

At the service, Dido bowed her head and muttered with the rest, but inside she was untouched. I don't belong here, perhaps I should go. They spoke of a daughter loved by her parents, a loving and sadly missed sister. Dido couldn't help but imagine this newcomer rifling through Joyce's records, her scents, stealing into Joyce's clothes. How death belittles us, if we become another's thoughts. Even the coffin looked too small to hold Joyce. In the graveyard, she remained at the rear, while the press of relatives – father and mother, brothers, sisters, uncles, aunts, nephews and nieces – blackened the view. After the prayers, she made to leave, but her movement was misconstrued and charitable backs made a path to the grave. Petals slid between the dirt where they had thrown roses on the coffin. Lilies had been Joyce's favourite. Didn't they know? Dido had brought her own posy, silky cream tubes. She sniffed. They had obviously been forced in this English clime, for there was no smell. Or rather, there was no fragrance. They smelt of green things, alive, pushing. She dropped them, turned and left.

The weight of families pressed on her. How jealous they were – of everything in heart-shot, like black holes in space hugging the world to their core. Everything of consequence was done in families. Joyce had started none, so life went back a step: her parents must reclaim her. Look, she wanted to say, I'm here too, touch me and I'll cry. But no, being only a friend's, her grief was unofficial. As though the only love worth the name was one that made, or could have made, more bloody families. Drivel.

You're an only child, she reminded herself, daughter of only children. Don't be bitter. For thirty years you've had her soul. Let them keep the bones.

As she was getting into her car, one of the brothers hurried to delay her. 'Thank you so much for coming,' he said.

'Oh,' she replied. She stumbled a bit. 'You must thank your parents for me.'

'Thank them?'

'For their help.' She realised she had put her foot in it, treading on family property. 'With the arrangements, I mean.'

The brother looked taken aback. Then he smiled – ministeringly, she thought. This must be the one who studied himself for orders. 'You'll have to forgive Father,' he said. 'Difficult circumstances, I'm sure you understand. She was his darling, you know. He never quite got over her running away like that.'

His darling – how quaint. Then: I suppose they blame me for her running away too.

'Don't lose touch,' he said as she closed her car door. 'There's so much we'd like to know. We got her letters, of course, but we never really knew her. Was she happy?' He asked this through the half-open window.

'Deliriously,' said Dido and drove off.

England she hardly recognised. Everyone was suddenly so much taller. Inside, she feared she found them mean, a nation guarding from its bungalows a past as remote as Camelot. She was reminded of those Arab peasants who, haggling in building sites, boast of Baghdad. Everywhere there were rules: no tea without a bun, buns come with jam. It was as though they had run out of people to be better than: and, still lauding themselves, had only each other to lord over.

Oh, Joyce had been aware of it all, it would have come as no surprise to Joyce. She addressed her letters home, 'c/o The Country Club, Thatcherite Britain, north-west corner of Europe'. Always the rebel – that true species of rebel who dreams the clock will stop, not jump ten paces forward.

She took to the moors, the sparse expanse of sheep and tree lines. When she stopped at a pub ('No bar food after two') she found herself gazing at a landscape on the wall. It was a typical scene: a lonely cottage in a steep vale, the hanging moors encroaching. She was a town-girl herself, brought up in Victorian suburbs that had been drained by the war. But she felt strangely drawn to that cottage – atavistically, as if to an ancestral home. She was not ashamed of her life. She had vied in a man's world to teach mathematics to girls and had always managed to support herself (and Joyce when necessary) in reasonable comfort. Suddenly, she wondered was it true – or had she been living in someone else's view? She felt fragile inside, isolated, as though everyone she had known had moved on up the hill. From their vantage point, they watched her now, in her quaint surroundings, still part of the scenery, still down in the vale.

She continued on the road, and found herself driving inevitably westwards until, breeching a final scar, she was stopped by the revelation of Giggleswick. She had forgotten she remembered this sight. There was the railway viaduct, the green dome of the school chapel, the old parish church, its tumbled acre. The sun reflected on limestone buildings, the beck meandered through levelled fields. Houses reached up to meet the moor and where they did the wild mountain became Constitution Hill. She walked by the beck and, yes, the ducks were still there and the trees were the same, or gave roughly the same shade. The girls who called from the playing fields called in familiar tones the old cries. And that bench there, that was the bench where she and Joyce first had understood.

A country is never so constant as in the mind of an exile. Shudders and blows await her return. But the rate of change is not universal. Villages that have grown up around old schools seem enhanced by time, like walls with ivy, and not ravaged by its passing. All those school bells ringing the classes, the classes themselves divided into quarter-hours by the tolling parish clock – how odd that so much time, recorded so meticulously, should lead to a sense of timelessness, rest.

She sat on the bench by the beck and, as though preserved in its flow, the memories came flooding. How Hobson, the school padre, MacNamara's friend, had made up to Joyce and how inseparable they were regarded: Hobson's Joyce, the schoolgirls called her. Then the tears, which seemed unaccountable at the time, when Joyce told Dido she was engaged. They sat on the bench while evening fell about them. Birds chirped in the hedges, the beck purled on. When the shadows reached them their fingers had touched and when Dido looked into Joyce's eyes, for the first time she knew that she looked where she loved. They kissed that night in the shade of that oak.

The banns went up. Hobson was cock of the walk for a week. But where was Joyce? She had disappeared. Rumour spread that she had returned Hobson's ring, and her father, the rector, had locked her away in the rectory tower. The village buzzed with anticipation – and when it was learned that a hidden hand had freed the captive, everyone assumed a secret suitor had intervened. The postmistress awaited a postmark from Gretna Green. But it was months later that news arrived: Joyce had taken ship to Africa. She was in Cape Town, six thousand miles away. Her father denounced her. Hobson damned her. MacNamara shook his head. But how surprised they all were when Dido announced her resignation. 'But where will you go?' asked the young MacNamara. 'Africa,' she answered blithely.

Everywhere she looked, everywhere she turned, Joyce was just round the corner. There was a house for sale. She didn't take much notice of it, just decided on the spot that she would buy it. She could settle here, as nowhere else, in the magical village where they'd met.

The telephone rang. 'Hello?' she said. Nothing. How bare was the hall without furniture, like a tunnel, a cave, leading nowhere. Outside the starlings were squabbling, the sparrows got on with it, winter lowered. But inside, the world seemed at bay. She realised she had let the phone dangle by its wire. 'Hello?' she said again. Still nothing. She replaced the receiver.

It was odd living in a house with so little furniture. However, she refused to buy anything new. Insurance and pensions didn't amount to much in this new Britain. Besides, the furniture delayed in Hartlepool had been gathered by both of them. Joyce had decorated the edges. Why should she pay for new and silent stuff when she had reverberant armchairs of her own?

Most of all she missed her music. She had all their records, Joyce's and hers, but the gramophone was in Hartlepool. One of their great joys had been to sing together. When they did the housework, their home rang with scales and arpeggios, ever more challenging, more devilish, and they might often conduct an entire conversation *recitativo*. Now, as she went about the day's business, she would try a few bars, a snatch of an aria or a chorus they had liked. But the house wouldn't echo and her voice sounded shrill. She soon stopped.

She telephoned to Hartlepool almost daily, but there was always some equivocation from the other end, some story that never approached an explanation. 'Madam is insured,' the man said. But what had insurance to do with it? She needed that furniture, those particular atoms, each one and every one. How else might she enghost this house with Joyce? How else to make it home?

For walking through the village, she realised its magic had not endured. It was as though that first torrent of memories when she sat by the beck had drained it of evocation. Or else her physicality, grossly as it had in the Gulf, killed it. It wasn't that she could not remember. The way she remembered was different. When she passed the tower-room of the rectory, she recounted facts. That tree was a bush then. Up drainpipe. Abrasion on knee. Knocked on window. Surprise on her face. Handed key. She kissed goodbye. A bi-labial click.

Incidents from her past were no longer points on a line on which she still travelled. That journey had ended; in mid-breath it had terminated with a sudden inexplicable fender in the desert. Our life is a narrative, whose past explains the present. And the memories she had were so happy, so outrageously lovely, they could have nothing to do with the paucity of today. Joyce came to seem like an invention, the confabulation of an unhappy mind.

She began to query details. For instance, one afternoon she replaced the telephone and the question from nowhere occurred to her: why was she christened Dido? Her father had been interested in Roman history, she knew; but to lumber a child with so different a name . . . Schoolgirls east and west, black, brown and Caucasian, had nicknamed her 'Dildo'. Besides, if her father was so interested in Roman history, why was she named for a Carthaginian queen? Or was she? Could it be, perhaps, that she was named for some other Dido, famous in some other field, whereof her father knew but she was unaware? Questions like this vexed her.

At night she still gazed at Joyce's picture. But she no longer was certain of the face. Sometimes, she caught herself wondering who it was supposed to be. Is that me? Of course, a moment's recollection brought Joyce's name, but then she might wonder who was this Joyce-person anyway. Tantalising seconds would pass before the force of truth prevailed.

Joyce, Joyce, Joyce – the confabulation of an unhappy mind. It was a short step to see Joyce not as the product, but as the cause of this unhappiness.

She did not choose to think ill of the dead, but if she was

truthful Dido had to admit Joyce's was a frivolous life. Her flippancy with money, amazing trust in pseudo-scientific books, fads in the kitchen, quasi-mystical therapies based on colour or sound. Frivolity of course is close to joy, and Dido had not begrudged Joyce her enthusiasms. In an odd way it was rather fun to dip into them of an evening. After a day's trigonometry at school, her fads in the home were like a soft mattress: easing to the back if not strictly wise. Dido had always sought equality in their life. But she could not help doubting if in her efforts that everything should be fair, shared equally, the good and the bad, Joyce never carrying an unequal burden, she hadn't deprived herself of her own just moiety of pleasure. When she carved the meat her plate held the fattier, grislier slice. She chose for herself the cup with the crack. Her own wardrobe was a dull backdrop to Joyce's originality. Strangers talked to Joyce in the street, shop-girls indulged her, but nobody noticed Dido. They complimented her soprano, while Dido's was considered too full, too *bel canto*. People assumed Dido was the stronger one, but it was Joyce who had willed her that way. God help Joyce if Dido goes first, they used to say. But good old Dido can look after herself. In effect, she had become the uglier straight one who remembered the bills. Instead of affinity, there was contrast. Where she had believed in equality, she had been forced into opposition. It just wasn't fair. She hadn't wanted it that way. Why had Joyce done this to her?

And then, having had her way, having enjoyed her fads, having rearranged Dido's molecules even, she had the cheek to up sticks and die. Leaving what? Half a whole, this manikin of a she, to rattle alone on a planet. How could you leave me like this?

At terrible times, she despised Joyce and pictured her as a capricious genius who manipulated souls. Afterwards, she was rooted with guilt. She ached to remember something pleasant, to look at something she loved, but all she could do was feed the birds. The telephone rang, she picked it up, she said hello, replaced the receiver. Joyce, where are you?

She became more and more accustomed to the house the way it was. These were her records: there was no gramophone. This was the guests' room: nothing in it. This was the master: a single bed. This the sitting-room: a sofa but no chairs. The dining-room was here: six chairs but no table. The names of these rooms lost their descriptive value and became merely epithets divorced from function. Six diners might sit in the dining-room, two on carvers: but no one could dine.

She was brushing her hair one morning when, glancing at her reflection, she saw that the age-old struggle between mirror and heart had ended for her. The face that the glass returned was an exact reproduction of the soul inside. My hair is like a German helmet, my face a public yashmak. The kaftan I wear is the chintzy cover of a chair that's losing its stuffing. She put down the mirror and cut some bread: the birds still had to be fed.

She worried her mind might follow her body, and to keep senility at bay, she took to proving mathematical theorems. A couple a day to begin with, then with practice more and more, figuring the equations in her mind's eye as physically she counted the birds.

How reliable was science, like an old-fashioned nurse or the Queen Mother. As a child she had wondered where had it all come from, who made the world. God had seemed inevitable then, like her father's coming home caused tea in the evening. But to the growing scientific mind, his theological innascibility made nonsense of God as an explanation. Though she ceased to believe, she did not consider herself irreligious. As far as she was concerned, the truly religious were those who were driven to enquire of the world: the irreligious asked nothing, merely followed the precedent of family, tribe, country. The cross that Dido bore was the burden all atheists carry: that driven to enquire by religious impulse, she had enquired and found nothing.

Yet she was struck by such eternals as the laws of indices, the transcendental number *pi*. They were truths to which the world conformed, yet they were not of the world. They came from beyond. As truths they were odd, intangible . . . having no actuality, no entelechy, requiring nothing to exist to be counted by them, but existing nonetheless, in a kind of god-like dispassion. They had a wonder about them, the wonder of religion, if not its solace.

At night she watched the stars, tracing the trivial constellations, and recalled Pythagoras's theorum. She shivered amongst all those shapes to know that before ever there was a triangle, before there were points or planes or units of measure, before even there was a universe in which shapes could exist, that theorem had held good. She muttered it under her breath: the square on the hypotenuse of a right-angled triangle is equal to the sum of the squares on the other two sides. She sounded not like the teacher she had been, nor any of the girls she had taught: in her voice was the murmur of devotion.

The Pythagoreans had heard music in the stars. But music was a long time ago now. As remote in time as the stars in space.

Joyce had toyed with astrology; but in her own way she too believed in the stars. They in their space were science's workshop. But the stars were hard and beneath their rays she felt exposed. For what was love, in scientific terms, but a nursery for the purposeful gene? Was that the answer? Their love was a kind of imaginary number, handy for calculations, but ultimately without substance.

How many women have you loved? The square root of minus one.

The moon rose. In Africa they had taken the moon for their cynosure. As their periods came together, Joyce had called it a sign from the ancient goddess herself that their union was blessed. But Dido did not remember Africa: instead she counted the seconds for the moon's reflected light to reach the earth. One two three four five . . .

A leaf fluttered from a tree by her terrace as she paced one morning, and she watched fascinated its intricate flight till it landed precisely on the tip of her toe. She was certain she could have felt nothing physically, yet its fall hit her with the force of revelation. So banal an encounter – leaf on shoe – it must happen a thousand times each day. Wherever trees are deciduous, in every temperate zone, leaves fall, feet move. Yet if she recounted the twists of cause and effect that had led to this rendezvous her mind must swim with the improbability of it. Why was she here, why had she chosen this morning to pace her terrace? Why this garden, this house, why England? Why was she born a European? Why had mankind come down from the trees for leaves to fall on their toes? So many causes, so many effects. And the tree itself – who planted it, when, why there? How many false starts, stops and goes, before nature hit on the notion of trees losing leaves in winter? The wonder of it was staggering. And was it all planned from the beginning, from that first explosion sixteen billion years ago when the constituent parts of nothing – an equal eternity of positive and negative – exploded into matter and time began? Time governed by the eternal rules, a ceaseless line of cause and effect, that decreed a galaxy and a sun on its rim, with a planet that circles at a temperate distance and on that planet and on this day, at this destined time, on this inevitable morning, Dido Poynings shall walk on her terrace and a leaf shall tip on her toe?

It was all so marvellous, so wonderous, all so utterly pointless. Who cares? she screamed, Who cares, who cares, who cares?

Only the innocent scream out loud. In the throbbing garden the only noise was the distant ringing of the phone.

An ugly dream recurred in her sleep. In this dream her world was shattering – not figuratively but literally. Her horizons were like glass pictures and the glass shattered. The shards did not fall, but disappeared into nothing. And with her horizons went the feelings of things: love, hate, history, everything – all disappeared with the shattering glass. And when all the glass had gone, she stood alone, not on the earth but on a planet that circled a sun, and it would do so till it didn't.

When she remembered this dream a panic would come. There was a buzz behind her eyes, an interference, as from an untuned television. Her head ached, and she felt not flushed not chilled, but in between; not good not bad, but stopped in the exact mathematical mean. She feared for her identity, the I who willed the self. She didn't walk, but was walked, didn't sleep but was slumbered. There is no passive voice to the verb 'to be', but that was how she felt. Experience without agency, effect without cause, Dido minus Joyce: once I was but now I am been. She felt as though she was still in that waiting-room, waiting six hours, as they pulled out tubes and injected Valium, waiting for Joyce to die.

It helped if she kept busy. That's why she was so diligent about feeding the birds. It even helped just answering the phone.

*

One evening, the telephone rang when she was half-way up the stairs, on her way to bed. This was unusual. The hoaxer had never phoned at night before. On the other hand, it could hardly be news from Hartlepool. The phone kept ringing, but it might stop at any moment. She trembled between decisions. Her body was directed up the stairs, her face looked back over her shoulder. This is ridiculous, she chided. She frowned, then padded down the stairs. She found the switch in the hall, lifted the receiver. But for once she did not say anything. She waited.

There was nothing at the other end, only the usual breath. Not quite a wheeze, she decided, though the voice struggled for air. Dido waited, holding the receiver pressed to her ear. The church clock struck an hour. There was something different about the breathing. It sounded almost familiar. Suddenly Dido was struck with the certainty, more than a certainty, or rather worse, it was like a terror, a terrible certainty that the voice at the other end was about to speak. She didn't know what, and she couldn't tell why, but she slammed the receiver down on its stand. She stood, gripping herself, stock-still. The hall felt unbearably cold. Her cheeks were flushed like pokers. She remembered she was in her nightdress, on the bare boards, under the bulb. She closed her eyes, but she could not let go. The breathing had sounded so familiar, so unutterably familiar. 'Oh Joyce,' she said finally. She bit her lip, but this did not stop the tears.

And how she cried. 'Oh, Joyce, my Joyce, my Joyce!'

The ugly dreams ceased after that and the meanness of science had gone.

Some weeks afterwards, she was returning from the village bakery, when she noticed that her side gate was ajar. She was incensed. Someone had crept down the ginnel, violated her domain. Worse, the sneak had left the gate open. The birds, she thought, they might have escaped! She calmed herself. This was silly. She looked in. Brogues, corduroys, tweed jacket: it was MacNamara. He was peeping through the kitchen window. The gate creaked as Dido closed it.

'Och, there you are,' said MacNamara.

'Good morning,' said Dido testily.

'I was passing and I thought I'd call, like. Feared I'd missed you there.'

All so pleasant, affable, as though he hadn't been caught trespassing. 'I can't invite you in,' she warned. 'There's rather a rush on this morning.'

'Not to worry.' They stood facing each other on the terrace. 'The thing is, there's a hockey do on at the school Saturday next. Senior team versus an old girl get-up, that manner of thing. Ah, sure being the doctor they expect you to show your face. I was thinking you might fancy a visit yourself. Back to the old school and all that. Might have a bite to eat afterwards. What do you say?'

'Do you mean this coming Saturday?' She shifted the weight of the parcels in her hand. If she edged towards the hall window, might she still catch the phone if it rang? Get rid of him, she resolved.

'If you've nothing planned, of course. Tell you what, I'll give you a tinkle nearer the day. By the by, I've had a thought about the hooligans.'

'Hooligans?'

'The telephone hoaxers, of course.'

'Oh.' The birds were complaining in the holly tree. They must be hungry.

'Did you ever think of having your number changed? That'd fox them. That'd put a short end to their larking.'

Dido relented her ill-humour long enough to consider the suggestion. 'Actually,' she said, 'the calls have stopped.

Yes, I haven't had a call in over a month. They must have tired of the joke.'

'Glad to hear it,' said MacNamara.

'Sorry, but I will have to get on.'

'I'll give you a tinkle, so. Towards the weekend.'

'Tinkle?'

'About the hockey.'

'Yes. Do.'

To Dido this exchange held the finality of farewell. But MacNamara made no motion of leaving. He rubbed his hands together. 'Wintry weather,' he remarked, then took a liberal lungful of the garden air. He gestured to the vista before them. You could see the old school chapel on its gritstone hillock peeking through the bare trees. 'Still,' he said cheerily, ''tis a grand garden you have.'

Garden, thought Dido: lawn, shrubs, trees, sky on top. Birds expecting their feed.

'And 'tis no accident 'tis grand. The man who had the place before you took a keen interest in the garden. He had a gardener, even. Young fella. Lived in. Leastways, we all took him for the gardener. Turned out though – only on his say-so, mind – that he was a mite more than any gardener you or I might employ.'

Why is he telling me this, wondered Dido. It was December and the days were far too short for prattling about nothing.

MacNamara persisted. 'I've no wish to speak out of turn, especially as regards the dead. For the man died, do you see, the man who owned the place before you. But the young fella maintained they were – how shall I put it? On terms a good deal closer than anyone suspected. Och, it was the talk of the village.'

'Well?' said Dido. Her toes tapped on the flags.

'Well, there was nothing in the will about it. What could

[79]

anyone do? He had to pack his bags and off he went – with something of a flea in his ear. Och, sure no relative would be pleased to be told a thing like that. After the death and all. However. Trouble was this young fella kept pestering the relatives. He couldn't accept the loss, you see. Couldn't come to terms with it. You know the pond below?'

He was squinting at the far corner. 'Pond?' said Dido.

'Down below.'

'There's no pond in my garden.'

'Exactly,' said MacNamara. 'But there's a hole there where a pond should be.'

He seemed delighted with his logic. 'I really don't see – ' said Dido.

'Turns out he had started a pond, the young fella had, and he wanted to finish it, do you see. Kept pestering the relatives to let him return. For what is a pond without water? A contour of the ground merely. It's still there, if you care to look. Or rather, it isn't. There's a vacancy in the ground where he wanted to build a pond. A memorial, do you see, to his friend. Became an obsession with him. Couldn't let it go. There's a word for it. Mourning syndrome, it's called.'

So that was it. Dido remembered that this trespasser was, by profession, a doctor. That was the purpose of this talk: delicately, genially to offer help.

'The death of a loved one affects different people different ways. Some folks can handle their mourning quite well.'

'They can?'

'Yourself, for instance.'

Dido surveyed the doctor, his profile only, for his face was still lapping up the garden view. You know nothing, she thought. I'm a mass of assumptions on your part. You look at me and you think of female disorders. You don't know that I couldn't cry. That now with the phone calls I don't need to. You don't know that I was losing Joyce, but now the phone rings every day. What do you know? You don't even know that I'm late for the birds.

The panic was returning. She needed to close her eyes. She needed to be busy. If only MacNamara would leave.

But no. 'They do these things better abroad,' he was saying. 'Funerals, I mean. Well, I don't know, but maybe you'll have seen it for yourself. On your travels, like. Out there, it's a piece of theatre. A public display of grief. Catharsis, to use the technical phrase. They have their big day, they're the centre of attention, and the bereaved – wife or mother, children, what have you – she – well, I mean he – they get it out of their system.'

'Indeed.'

'Societies, you know, less developed in our sense of the word, but closer, do you see, to maybe what's inside of them.'

How very thoughtful of him, thought Dido, to lecture her on social anthropology at this hour of the day. At any moment the phone might ring and she'd have this Irish oaf nosing into her onions.

'This country,' he said, 'I still feel we've a lot to learn.'

'Doubtless,' said Dido.

He faced her directly. 'It's not easy for – well, a friend, I know that. Just to let you know there's help available, should you need anyone.'

Go help the young fellow, Dido told him after he had gone. I have my birds.

As soon as she got inside she checked that the phone wasn't off the hook – she'd tipped it over once by accident and it had been off for three-quarters of an hour before she'd noticed. Then she went outside and deposited chunks of bread. She bought the bread specially now, good brown wholemeal stuff. Five loaves a day, the bakery kept them for her. Half a loaf at a time, which meant the birds had ten feeds a day, staggered through the daylight hours. It kept her in harness. The chunks were roughly one-inch cubes. She had arrived at this size through trial and error. It was just too heavy or awkward for the birds to fly away with in their beaks, just too small to occasion too much of a squabble. Consequently the birds could feed in relative peace while she could watch over them peacefully.

Once the chunks were dispersed, she hurried into the hall to keep watch through the window. She loved the hall now, with its walls and ceiling, and could not imagine why it had chilled her before. The phone was there and the garden window might have been specially designed for a conscientious governess. She had dragged the sofa in from the sitting-room. Nearby whined the electric fire. The phone gleamed on the floor beside it. How cosy was her nook. Home at last.

She picked up the receiver to listen to its purr. The dialling tone gave pleasant assurance. Then she watched out the window the squawking starlings, the apprehensive sparrows.

Sometimes another bird might intrude on this dichotomy. A crow might swoop: its giant shadow barely had time to form on the flags before it had lifted again, an entire chunk in its beak. Or it might actually land. Then it would stalk up to its chosen morsel, fix its claw imperiously on its centre, daring the slightest misrule. But Dido Poynings knew about crows. With her mortar-board and her black academicals she'd ruled over many a class, swooping on malcontents, corvine. I am Dido Poynings, she said, a crow who answers the phone.

She was so busy – an entire school in her garden – she felt light in her head. I'll float away one of these days, she told herself. At the same time, she was gripped by a physical

THE CROW WHO ANSWERED THE PHONE

happiness, a euphoria so strong she shook in its power. The weather was marvellous – sumptuously cold! And the rain when it fell was uniquely wet. The wind blew with the bitterness of fruits. The sun shone like a dozen moons. Was there ever a winter to match it? And at any moment the phone might ring. She trembled in premonition of its call.

Panic was kept at bay, but only generally. In moments, it sortied through her defences. Then, her every extremity would numb, while her mind buzzed with interference. If she waited long enough, she was returned to her dream. Everything was glass, shattering into nothing.

Feeding the birds might hinder this panic, but only the telephone calls could truly confront it. They were special. They came to her only. In coming they made her special.

The phone rang, not regularly but reliably. Dido lifted the receiver, pressed it to her ear. She didn't answer it any more, in the sense that she said hello or gave her number. She merely listened. And as soon as she was certain that the voice at the other end was about to speak, utter distinguishable sound: then she slammed the receiver down. On these occasions she was truly alive. She felt intemperate. Either she shivered with cold or she sweated with heat.

Sometimes she wondered why she didn't speak. At times she childishly dared herself. 'I am Dido Poynings,' she might say, 'a crow who answers the phone!' But in her heart she knew this was impossible. The world she inhabited had changed with the phone calls. She had found the secret door, and her garden was not driven by blind laws of science, but by the human power of desire. This was the world of mystery and sympathy, wound through subtly with magic, where actions became rites, whose observance alone ensured its continuity. Should she falter one inch in her step, alter one jot of her behaviour, the spell would shatter, and she would stand on a planet, alone as in her dream, circling a nearby star.

She had brought her bedding down from the master bedroom and she slept now on the sofa in the hall. Less comfortable, perhaps, and yet, with the coalman not delivering and the electric fire on the day long, it did make sense. Besides, it being January and the days growing longer, the birds of course were rising earlier. She didn't have time for traipsing up and down stairs. They needed breakfast. If she slept in her clothes it guaranteed an early start, and she could watch through the window the dawn reach over the garden trees, she could hear the chorus chirm its thanks.

She noticed that her gait was stiffer. Her knees didn't bend, her toes pressed against the roof of her shoes. She shuffled on the balls of her feet, as if she should be wearing slippers. When she looked at her legs she laughed. Calfs should grow into cows, she thought, but mine have turned into spindles. In the village she was consumed by a craving to shout out to everyone, to be known, to proclaim: 'I am Dido Poynings, a crow who answers the phone!' But the words came out as 'Five loaves of bread, please.'

Hartlepool no longer bothered her. Indeed, in her mind, it had become an exotic, forbidden place, far more inaccessible, improbable even, than any of the polygonal corners of the world where she had taught. When she thought of her furniture the details had faded. She had pictures, of course, but she could not picture them. If she tried, an image came of a cottage on the moors, the toppling hills encroaching. Panic lay that way. Better off by far with the faded patches.

There was so much to do. People didn't understand. She was leaving the bakery one morning when somebody called out her name.

'Dido! Is that you, Dido?'

She turned, but she could not recognise any of the faces. Flitting between the people she caught the shape of a woman. She knew that shape. Oh yes, unmistakable. In her Gossard Wonderbra, the eternal Sweater Girl. There you are, she said. She raised her hand in gentle salute. I'm over here, Joyce, shan't be long. But unaccountably Joyce wasn't there any more. Joyce? Panic struck through the chink. Joyce? Joyce? Bread spilled on the pavement. She collapsed in its midst. Joyce? Oh Joyce.

A hand touched her shoulder. She jerked her head wildly.

'Dido! You know I'd hardly recognise you. What have you been up to? You look the wraith of yourself.'

It was that man again. 'Oh,' said Dido. Oh dear, Oh dear.

'Here, let me help you.' The giant gloved hand reached under her shoulder and raised her to the human position.

'I'm so sorry,' she said.

'Not at all, not at all,' said MacNamara. 'The roads are fierce slippery this time of the year. They don't seem to salt them any more at all, I don't know why.'

Salt? No, that would be bad for the birds.

'Tell you one thing. I was a mite concerned the last day I visited. Is it coming together for you now?'

She tried to look round his shoulder, then wondered why. Was she looking for someone? Who was it now?

'Glad to hear it,' said MacNamara, though she did not believe she had spoken. 'And you're looking after yourself? I trust so, anyway. Looking a mite pale – round the edges, like. Are we feeding ourselves proper?'

She was waiting for somebody. Who was it again?

'The vittles are vital, as we say in the trade.' He had picked up the bread. 'Staff of life and all that, but don't neglect the protein. One cooked meal a day, at least. Do you hear me?'

[85]

She nodded quickly. MacNamara looked at his watch. A signal he would go? No. He leaned closer. He had secret information to impart. 'You're still missing Joyce.'

Joyce! Of course! But what did he know about Joyce? Any moment the phone might ring and here he was delaying her in the street. Her brain buzzed. She wanted to tell this man that she was Dido Poynings and that she was a crow who answered the phone. But her tongue insisted on some trite rationality. 'Yes,' she said, 'I think you're right.'

MacNamara straightened again. 'Time's the great healer. I could prescribe any amount of pills, but time's your man. You'll see.'

'Yes, that's right. Time to go.' She adventured a smile.

His face looked doubtful again. 'Tell you what. There's a concert on at the school.'

Here we go.

'Sunday next. School choir, you know the way it is. Don't say anything now, yea or nay. I'll telephone during the week. But think on. 'Twould do you the world.'

'Thank you,' said Dido.

'Shame about Christmas and all.'

'Christmas?'

'Maybe next year you won't be so busy.'

Oh dear, won't I?

'Silly, two old friends spending the festivities alone like that. So think on.'

'Yes, I'll certainly think on.'

'Anyway. I'll have to be on my way. Love to chatter and all that. But – something of a rush on. Half the county's in the surgery with the flu. As though I had some magic potion. I'll phone.'

'Phone, yes.'

He was already half-way down the street. He had a stiff

arm raised in farewell. As though he was supporting something, she thought.

She hurried home, back to the cosy nook in the hall. She fed the birds. The phone would ring. In touch.

The explosion came one Friday afternoon.

Dido had fed the birds, she was supervising them through the hall window. The starlings were up to their tricks again and she'd just rapped a warning when the phone rang. She was momentarily divided – the birds required her every vigilance – but only momentarily: the call of the phone was undeniable. She lifted the receiver.

Just as she did so, there was an almighty screeching and chattering outside which ended as suddenly as it had begun and a sharp thin silence stung the air. Dido strained to see what was happening. There wasn't a bird in sight. The bread lay scorned on the flags. Then suddenly, so fast she barely had time to register it, a hawk crashed into the holly tree, swept out again, all in one movement, all of a piece, except when it swept out, it had a sparrow in its beak.

Dido was shaking. She did not know how to feel. She had lost one of her birds, but it had been a magnificent sight. The poor sparrow. And now she had hawks to contend with. How should she accommodate hawks in her garden? Questions and quandaries surged through her mind. She wanted to wrap her face in her hands, dam this turbulence, when in doing so, she realised that one of her hands still held the telephone. It was pressed against her ear. And there was a voice at the other end, and the voice was speaking, making distinguishable sound. She closed her eyes. Oh my God, she thought. This is unbearable.

'Russell?' said the voice. 'Is that you, Russell? . . . Russell? . . . Russell? . . .'

Russell.

She exploded. She cried. She stamped. She did human things. She shouted out how cruel they were. They had taken her Joyce, the love from her life, they'd taken her memories and half of her years, they'd even taken half her furniture and lost it in Hartlepool – damn them to hell, but they'd stooped so low as to steal one of her sparrows: now they must take her telephone calls. It was beyond cruelty. I am Dido Poynings, a crow who answers the phone! My home is Jerusalem, centre of the world! Except it wasn't true. All along it had been some piddling mistake. There was an idiot abroad giving out the wrong number. His name was Russell. What was wrong with him? Was he mad? Some sort of maniac, giving the wrong number. It was enough to make your blood boil. Enough to make you cry salt tears. No, no, no! She would not suffer this. It was too too much. She would suffer this no more . . .

These barkings endured for an interval, a period of time that could be measured in hours, multiples of seconds, themselves arbitrary units conventionally measured by the movement of heavenly bodies, or as at Greenwich by the earth's rotation around the sun, or most ingeniously of all by the frequency of radiation emitted by caesium as its atoms decay. Time. It passed. And when it had, she was no longer in the hall. She wasn't anywhere really. She stood not on the earth but on a planet that circled the sun. It would do so till it didn't. The panic approached, but her last defences had fallen, and it did not come to her as panic, but as a generous victor, bringing end. Entropy was general, in fulfilment of thermodynamic law.

*

That noise, that was the phone ringing. When you picked it up, you said hello.

'Dido?' came the voice from the other end.

'Hello,' she said.

'Ah, there you are, Dido. MacNamara here.'

She waited.

'Er – sorry to trouble you this late. I called around, but there was no answer. Yet I saw a light was on.'

Light, she thought. You saw it tonight, but in a year someone six billion miles away will watch it pass.

'Only it's about this concert. You know, the school and all that. On Sunday. I wondered if you'd made up your mind at all.'

Mind: that which thinks, knows, feels, wills. Apparently you could make it up.

'Whether you wanted to go.'

She'd been going all her life. Never faced up to trouble really, never squarely. A curt retort and you never heard of me again. But that was all over. She need never go again, never move from this hall even. Finished. *Terminus* in Latin. QED in maths.

'Dido?'

'Yes?'

A sigh of relief. 'I thought you'd gone.'

'No, still here.'

'I wouldn't trouble you, only there's a question of tickets.'

The things this man can be troubled by. She troubled herself with a response and said, 'No, afraid I'm rather busy on Sunday.'

He sounded strangely jealous. 'I know you're busy, Dido. Your line's forever engaged.'

'They're not for me. They're calls for Russell.'

'Russell? Who's Russell?'

She was about to tell him it didn't matter, but he interrupted.

'Now, there's a thing. The man who had the house before you, his name was Russell. Fancy that. Russell something or other.'

She finally understood. It's the young fellow, of course. It was the gardener phoning all along. He's looking for his friend, his lover who died. Two years, my God, and he still – and he still – he phones because he can't let go. It's the mourning syndrome.

'Wait a minute, wait a minute.' MacNamara was smelling a rat. 'Are you still getting those strange telephone calls? I thought you said they'd stopped?'

'They have now.'

'Dido, are you all right?'

'It really doesn't matter.'

MacNamara mumbled on. How worried the man sounded. 'Look, about next Sunday. I don't want to insist, Dido, but it really is a shame. They'll be singing some of those old Purcell songs we all used to sing. Our party piece, remember?'

Was this man never to be satisfied?

'Of course you remember. From *Dido and Aeneas*. It was your mother's favourite opera. You used to say she named you for it.'

Dido and who, did you say? Dido and what?

Then, to her surprise, there came down the phone a warbling of poetry. '*Shake the cloud from off your brow . . .*' MacNamara was singing!

Dido and Aeneas. Yes, there was something about that music. It had been their party piece. She had sung Dido's part, of course. Joyce was Belinda. Poor old Hobson with his squeaky voice had to battle with Aeneas's bass baritone. Kettle's on the Hobson, they had called him. And Mac-

Namara had sung – no, he hadn't sung at all, but had pranced about in front of them, pretending to conduct. If she tried, she could picture them now. All four walking down the lane, Hobson squeaking determinedly, Mac-Namara waving his hand in front, Joyce with her hand in Dido's pocket, and the feeling of her smiling beside her. *'Ah, Belinda,'* she heard herself sigh. *'Ah, ah, ah, Belinda . . .'*

'I am pressed with torment,' sang MacNamara, *'not to be confessed.'* He had taken her sigh for his cue to continue. *'Peace and I are strangers grown . . .'*

How silly he sounded, thought Dido, cranking out his absurd falsetto over the phone. And yet considerate, too. The music, when she remembered it, was light and at the same time sad: no wonder it had been their favourite. Who would expect so purely mathematical an art so nearly to fulfil our emotions? Listening to his singing, she could almost see the music in front of her, and in its progressions she read the bones of life: a measure of prediction, a measure of surprise. She really didn't want this to happen, she really wanted it to stop. But the music had caught hold of her mind and everywhere she turned she faced the determined fugue, the accidental sharp. Stop it! Stop it! I don't wish to go on. But it wouldn't stop, no matter how she tried, because she loved Joyce and Joyce had loved to sing. Suddenly, she wanted too to sing, to let go finally her voice in the air; and to her wonder she heard the strain of her soprano echoing down the line: *'I am anguished till my grief is known; yet would not, yet would not, yet would not have guessed it.'*

'Grief increases by concealing,' sang MacNamara in return, taking Belinda's part in the recitative.

'Mine admits of no revealing.' She was only half-singing, the rest was stutter and breath. And yes, it was true. Grief

does increase with concealing. It came to her suddenly that was what this famous mourning syndrome was all about. You can't let go, because nobody knows you have it.

'Dido, if I called round at seven, we could drive to the school. It wouldn't do any harm.'

He sounded so kind, he was making her cry. 'It's true,' she said. 'It does increase with concealing.'

'I know,' said MacNamara. 'Shall I call, Dido, at seven?'

'Please,' she said before she could interrupt herself. 'Yes please.'

Dido Poynings strolls through the garden. The day is beautiful. She does not believe she can remember a morning so rare, the air as crisp as the earth beneath her, the sun almost bursting so brilliantly it shines. There is a wild patch of woodland towards the bottom, and there snowdrops and crocuses and daffodils wave on the banks. Earlier she watched the sun glint on the squat green dome of the school chapel, visible starkly through the trees. It has disappeared now, within hours, hidden behind foliage newly unfurled. Spring is everywhere.

A crow caws above and she stops to watch the rookery. For a while she believed she was a crow. A healthy dose of insanity, MacNamara calls it. That too makes her happy, for no one goes mad because they did not love. All this business of science and God. Nature is what is, not what should be. And if there is a God, then love – which alone transcends the inches – then love is holy. That settles it. She has loved and has looked where she loved and knowing this she knows she is special.

As she walks up the lawn towards the terrace and the kitchen door, she can hear the telephone ringing inside. She knows who it will be. And she knows what she will say.

She'll explain her provenance, 'My name is Dido Poynings,' and she'll speak about the garden. For what is a garden without a pond? Even with a pond, she'll need someone to care for it. If she can, she'll help the boy with his grief.

She smiles to herself. If you wanted, you could write it like a sum:

$$present + purpose = future.$$

She's worried momentarily. By transposition, that would mean that the present equals the future minus a purpose. Does that make sense?

Silly maths, she thinks. Silly me.

She is still smiling when she picks up the phone.

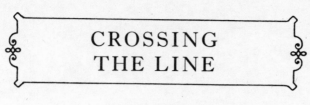

CROSSING THE LINE

Tony Peake

It was my father who taught me about crossing the line.

Usually, where I was concerned, his work was a cushion against intrusion.

'Don't disturb your father, dear. He's working.'

Or: 'Not now, boy. Can't you see I'm busy?'

All the more surprising, then, that on my eleventh birthday he should ask me if, as a treat, I'd like to visit the studio.

'You mean to watch you making a film?'

I could hardly believe my ears.

'Not me. I don't have anything in production at present. But there'll be something you can watch.'

My mother dressed me for the visit with more than customary care, and when my wardrobe was complete, stood behind me to check her handiwork in the glass. I can see the picture we made even now: the child in sandals, gartered socks, khaki shorts, short-sleeved shirt and tie, his hair as ordered as his clothes, and behind him, thrown like a shadow against the wall, the worried outline of his mother, fussing with his collar.

'Excited?'

My father never asked me how I felt, and his question – fired as we swept through the studio gates – reduced me to speechlessness.

'Come on, boy! Lost your tongue?'

I'd been a boy to him for as long as I could remember: always boy, never Lawrence.

'Yes, sir.'

In my nervousness, I reverted to the hierarchical grammar of school.

My father raised an eyebrow; then, swinging the car to a standstill, said curtly: 'I've got some things I need to look over. John will take you round.'

John turned out to be a trainee electrician, resentful of his status as a menial, and it was with barely concealed impatience that he led me through the offices, the editing suites, the storage vaults, before abandoning me on Sound Stage One, where they were indeed in the process of shooting a film.

Terrified that I might knock something over, or inadvertently step into the limelight, I huddled in the lea of a tea trolley and watched fascinated as a man kicked in a door, grabbed hold of a woman as terrified as me, and struck her across the face. This action he repeated twenty times, until someone shouted 'Take Five!' and my father appeared on the set and siphoned the woman into conversation.

I approached silently, cautiously, still scared that I might stray into forbidden territory.

'Harry! You should have told me!' Close up, there was a shocking coarseness about the woman's features.

'Your eyes, your nose, your mouth. But *twice* as handsome. No wonder you're jealous!'

I found myself the unwelcome focus of a two-fold scrutiny: his and hers.

'So, my young Adonis!' Her voice was as fulsome as her make-up. 'It wasn't too boring? The filming?'

The intensity of their joint gaze prompted me into an unusually voluble response.

'It was very interesting,' I stammered, 'though I didn't understand why, after the man had hit you, and they'd moved the cameras to the other side of the set, why you both changed places, I mean, isn't that going to look odd?'

'Intelligent, too!' The actress chose not to answer my question, but to turn it into a compliment designed more for my father's benefit than mine.

My father, however, took the question at face value, and for the first time in my life, treated an utterance of mine as worthy of detailed reply.

'It's called crossing the line,' he said. 'If the camera changes its relationship to the actors, then unless the actors adjust themselves to accommodate that change of relationship, it will look on screen as if they are coming at each other from the wrong direction.'

He drew an explanatory diagram with the toe of his shoe in the sawdust we happened to be standing on, then rubbed it out and consulted his watch.

'But we'd better be going. You know how your mother worries.'

And to the actress, *sotto voce*: 'I'll ring you later.'

I have often thought, in the years since then, of the myriad lines that were in fact crossed that afternoon – and of how some lines, once crossed, do not re-establish the reality that was there before, but forge a new one. I certainly never looked at my father in the same way again. The boy had glimpsed the man.

Six years later. I am seventeen, and again I stand before my mother's mirror. This time, though, the uniform is different. This time I am wearing one of my mother's dresses: the green velvet with the plunging back.

I strike a pose and run a dramatic hand through my hair. I suck in my cheeks and lower my eyes. I bat my eyelashes. Then, closing my eyes, I let my mind run the sequence it keeps for occasions like these: a door is kicked in, a man strikes me across the face, one, two, ten, twenty times; then, miraculously, I am safe in a stranger's arms, a tall, dark, handsome stranger who smells of my father.

A door bangs somewhere, and I struggle out of the dress. By the time my mother enters the room, I am innocuous again, normal again, in T-shirt and shorts.

She sits heavily on the bed and dabs at the back of her neck with a minuscule square of lace.

'How is he?' I ask.

Suddenly she is crying. 'I don't think it will be long now. The doctors won't say, of course, but I can tell from his eyes.' The square of lace is unequal to the task demanded of it, and she casts it aside. I hand her my own more manly handkerchief. She clutches my wrist.

'I know you've had your differences,' she says. 'I know he's a difficult man. But he loves you really. You're very alike. If only you could see it. Please visit him. Otherwise you'll live to regret it. I know you will.'

Who directs me to play the scene this way? I'm not sure. But when I visit him, I go not as myself, but fulsomely, as her. I invest in my first wig, a selection of make-up, the dress, the nylons, the high heels. I stand by his bed and vamp him by sucking in my cheeks and batting my eye-lashes. The usual routine.

At first he doesn't notice me. When he does, a spasm of terror distorts his face.

'You!' he gasps.

Finally, as he realizes it isn't me at all, but her, he relaxes and fumbles for my hand.

'What?'

I need yet fear the way he is pulling me towards him. He

chuckles. At least, I think he chuckles. Air certainly passes through what is left of his lungs.

'What?' I repeat.

He has his mouth to my ear.

'I want you,' he whispers, 'to touch me. You know. Like you used to touch me. When we . . . You know.'

I am rescued by a nurse, who comes to take his temperature. I wait by the door, and as the nurse holds the thermometer between his lips, I notice that his hand is tracing a pattern on the sheets. It reminds me of the afternoon at the studio; how, with the toe of an immaculate shoe, he'd drawn that diagram in the dust.

'He should rest,' says the nurse.

'That's all right,' I say, forgetting to keep my voice falsetto. 'I was leaving anyway.'

On the way home, I stop at the public toilets I've recently discovered, the ones in the park, and fitting my cock to the hole in the partition, repeat my father's words.

'I want you,' I whisper, 'to touch me. Like you used to touch me. When we . . . You know.'

What I am given, on the other side of the divide, invisible yet intimate, is a stranger's tongue to bring me off at the moment my father dies. One coming. One going. Or so I discover later when I get home (having changed, I should add, into normal clothes) to find my mother being valiant in the kitchen.

'He's gone,' she informs me. 'They rang from the hospital. It was very peaceful, apparently. He just slipped away.'

At the crematorium I walked my mother down the aisle like a groom. I was her protector, her stalwart, her man.

'I may have lost my Harry,' she confided in the guests at the funeral tea, 'but at least I have Lawrence.' She was still on my arm – she didn't leave it all day – and one, two ten, twenty times she patted my wrist and said: 'At least I have Lawrence.'

On the mantelpiece, in a plastic bag inside an urn, stand my father's ashes: heavy, cold and silent.

That night, when I took her a cup of cocoa to help her sleep, she gestured slyly towards her cupboard: 'Which is your favourite?'

'I beg your pardon?'

'My dresses. Which suits you best?'

'You mean you know?'

'Of course.'

'And you don't mind?'

She giggled coquettishly. 'We've always been closer, you and I, than you and your father. He didn't understand you. Like never appreciates like. I want to see you. In the navy blue. The one with the collar.'

'Oh, Mum, I . . .'

But she was adamant. 'The navy blue. Go on.'

So I transformed myself for her into a younger version of herself, and pirouetted skittishly about the room while she settled into her pillows and watched me over the rim of her cup. Like pretending to be like.

As with the marriage that had preceded it, ours was rotten with deceit. She didn't mind that we shared her clothes – indeed, this she actively encouraged – but the fact that I might look outside the marriage for physical gratification of a kind she couldn't offer: this she found repugnant. If she saw a piece in the paper about a man arrested for indecency, or an account of the fight against Aids, she would draw my attention to it over supper, shaking her head and saying: 'So lucky to have you. So lucky you're not like that.'

Which meant, of course, that on the way to and from work – or in the evenings, instead of the French lessons I was supposed to be taking – I had to squeeze a lifetime of romance into a few stolen minutes. One, two, ten, twenty times a week I would allow some stranger (tall sometimes, dark sometimes, even – on occasion – handsome) to touch me. Like you used to touch me. When we . . . You know.

How long did this continue? All through my twenties, my thirties, and well into my forties – until, in fact, I was the age my father had been when he took me to the studios. When I looked in the mirror now, I saw what my mother had warned me against: that I was indeed my father's son. It was his face that frowned at me from the glass, his eyes that searched mine for the hope of difference. His nose, his mouth. Even his smell.

Kissing my mother on the forehead, I would leave her in front of the television and slip away. One, two, ten, twenty strokes of the hand – that was all it took. That and the scent of him. My scent. My father's scent. I was back in time for cocoa.

Lying alone in bed, my arm around the pillow, I would repeat the most he'd ever said to me.

'If the camera changes its relationship to the actors, then unless the actors adjust themselves to accommodate that change of relationship, it will look on screen as if they are coming at each other from the wrong direction.'

He'd been dead for twenty-five years, and I'd never mourned him, never missed him. Or so I told myself. And yet here he was, in the guise of myself, walking towards me across the years, eyebrows raised in ironic greeting.

'Mother,' I said. 'I think the time has come to scatter Father's ashes.'

[103]

'We weren't really suited,' she said. 'I tried to put a good face on it, but he was an angry man. Disaffected. I never gave him what he wanted.' She reached for my hand. 'I'm glad you're different.'

'That's not', I said, 'what you usually say.'

'Perhaps', she said, 'we live and learn.'

'So you agree then?'

'About what?'

'The ashes.'

'If you say so. Dust to dust.'

We both dressed in our Sunday best. She wore white. I wore a suit. There was a hill behind the studio where I knew my father had gone to be alone; he'd pointed it out the afternon he'd taken me to see the filming.

'Where are we going?' she asked. Now that she was nearing death herself, she didn't like surprises.

'To a place he knew. Where he could be himself.'

I parked the car just below the brow of the hill and helped my mother from her seat. Whilst she smoothed her dress, I lifted the ashes from the boot. I offered her my free arm and guided us to the top of the hill.

'Do you still miss him?' she asked.

'Did I ever?'

'Didn't you?'

I twisted the top off the urn and removed the plastic bag. The ashes had lost none of their baleful weight. I made a hole in the bag with my finger, widened the hole, then – in a single gesture – flung the ashes from me.

The wind did the rest. It took the ashes and blew them back in my face, and into my mother's hair, coating us paternally.

My mother raised an arm in protest.

I opened my mouth to laugh, and as I did so, bit on the gritty, continuing fact of myself.

'Confetti!' I laughed. 'So! To the marriage of true minds.'

'Come!' My mother had me urgently by the arm. 'I want to go home.'

'All right.' Suddenly it didn't hurt me to say it. 'I'll take you home. I'll take us both home. The two of us together. Just you and me. Made for each other.'

And giving her my right arm, I led her carefully to the car.

Still and for ever, it is my father who teaches me about crossing the line.

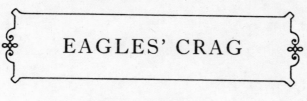

EAGLES' CRAG

Ronald Frame

To me, it is – it *was* – my golden time.

Edinburgh in the late Fifties. I was twenty-three, twenty-four. Never mind the sooty buildings, and the black cars in the cobbled streets, and the dark clothes, and the faces douce and smug by turns, and the prim manners of the place.

I was working on contract for the BBC in Glasgow writing scripts for a long-running radio serial a little in the style of Sir Walter Scott. Scott with a bit of gung-ho, *Boys' Own* adventure stuff thrown in. A weekly cliffhanger, with our panting heroine awaiting rescue from yet another impending calamity.

In those days, living in windy Edinburgh at the top of a round tower in the very heart of the Old Town, my head was a whirl of images and story-lines and cod-1640s dialogue. I looked down from my window and ignored the smoke and smog and the traffic in the narrow streets and saw instead the past being re-enacted, a past that was simultaneously violent and romantic to my mind's eye.

Perhaps my obsession had something to do with the strong sweet tea I survived on, which I drank in the Spartan Café just a few yards down the Royal Mile. I loved everything about my life. The steaming urn of Nessie's tea, the speed I was required to work at for my masters, having to stay awake until two or three in the morning typing up my completed script. I loved the creaking of the old floorboards in my room, which made me think I was on a sailing ship. I relished even the persistent cold, and the draughts blown up from the Firth of Forth which set the window frames rattling.

I was young and optimistic, I had my health, I had a job, I was living in a big city for the first time and commuting twice a week through to Glasgow in the west.

I felt above all my life was *necessary*.

My scripts were doctored by the serial's female producer in my absence, but even so there was a formal pretence that my opinion was of some weight, so I would attend a discussion of each script's merits and, more to the point, its longueurs and excesses. I even enjoyed the process of cutting down as whole pages, sometimes an entire scene, would be scribbled through and I scrawled OUT! OUT! down the margins in my copy.

Miss McGillivray, the name I always called her by to her face and to my colleagues, was the only woman producer I had encountered in my short radio life, and maybe I felt obliged to be chivalrous in conceding to her editorial suggestions. At any rate, I very seldom raised an objection. At our initial meeting I had unfortunately mistaken her for a secretary: she was in her forties, petite, with a tight perm of greying hair and a round face resembling for paleness a bun that hadn't cooked through properly, with submerged button eyes like dark currants and a small glacé cherry mouth that shrank and shrank when she was displeased. She wasn't an object of beauty, but she must have spent quite a bit of money on clothes – soft woollen separates, jersey suits and fine kid shoes, which seemed to contradict her reputation for unfeminine toughness – and invariably she cast behind her an elusive vapour trail of perfume that smelt of its own expensiveness, the sort that the good professional men's wives of Edinburgh with their charge-accounts would not have had the courage to buy for themselves.

I would return to Glasgow three days after our script session for the live transmission.

My prime reason for going, apart from being able to claim my full attendance allowance, was to ogle at our leading lady, Dolores Mitchell. I had no doubt that she was the most stylish woman, and perhaps the most beautiful, certainly the most striking, whom I had ever crossed paths with.

A long neck, ballerina features, fair hair delightfully straggling from its chignon roll. She wore cut-off Peter Pan slacks that were the fashion, and a blouse tucked tightly into the high waistband so that it pulled over her pop-up breasts. I admired everything about her appearance, and had fallen under the influence of that silky siren's voice. For the first few weeks she had almost entirely ignored me, with the result that when she did finally favour me with her regard, I felt that it was a recognition which I had positively *earned* for myself.

The change occurred without prior warning, quite suddenly. From failing to notice, she was now – by complete contrast – indulging me with smiles, bringing her cup of canteen tea over to my corner of the studio, positioning her chair so that she could hear everything I said to Miss McGillivray. She allowed me to offer her a cigarette, to light it even, to go chasing after ashtrays. I pushed in her chair for her or eased it back, I handed her her chinchilla cardigan jacket which she would drape over her shoulders, in the manner of true theatrical actresses. Between the read-through and the broadcast, over lunch, she would ask me some pertinent questions about radio technique; back in the studio she had me show her where to stand in relation to the microphone, enquiring as to the points at which I 'envisaged' the pauses coming in her speeches. I saw Miss McGillivray watching us from the control panel, darting looks over the rims of her glasses, and not at all approvingly; those were questions for *her*, of course, but I assumed that Dolores felt too intimidated to ask, as we all did. Maybe too Miss McGillivray didn't judge cliques to be wise policy in a continuous set-up like ours? But some things were only natural, I believed quite earnestly, they were *destined* to be, and if Dolores and I were to become friends, and conceivably even more than friends after a while . . .

I realised that I had to curb my fancies, to try to remember I couldn't always be up there in my turret of dreams. One day at a time, I told myself. But I couldn't wait for each recording day to come round in the week, when we cantered through the script at a rehearsal before getting down to the live broadcast in the late afternoon, for our expectant tea-time audience.

The degree of Dolores' friendliness varied from one Thursday to the next, and I never knew how I should find her. Was the tension of performance responsible, I wondered? I suppose now, with my distant overview of events, that there were only five or six Thursdays out of the twenty or so in which she featured when she allowed me to act the perfect gentleman with her, and those weren't consecutive. It's that which must account for my indecision at the time, why I was left screwing up my courage to ask her – would she care to join me for supper sometime, or dinner, or at the very least a drink? – and never getting to the bit. On the train journey home I would seem to see Dolores everywhere, even though I knew she was far too fine and glamorous for all those humdrum locations passing outside, she wasn't at all the type you expected to come across in a third-class compartment at nine or ten o'clock at night, with condensation like dirty netting at the windows. My ears would still be listening to that svelte honeyed voice, perfectly audible through the whistle blasts and the commotion of the wheels, 'Darling, just one more question . . .', '*Could* I ask you, would you mind most terribly if we changed just one *tiny* thing . . .'

With 'The Perils of Eagles' Crag' I lived in a world of my own manufacture, which belonged to no specific age. Historical authenticity wasn't my strong point, as Miss McGillivray appreciated but hadn't the time left over from her other ventures to do anything about; the scripts were littered with anachronisms for the mid-seventeenth century, which vigilant listeners wrote in to make their pedantic corrections to. But I didn't care, if Miss McGillivray didn't, I was too busy writing at white-hot speed, watching the nib of my pen as it raced across the page.

I forgot about the dangers to myself, in introducing so many into my plots.

I lived inside each of my characters in turn, with my head in the clouds, unable to register the real Edinburgh because I was imagining it as a place of ready adventure and heroism and depravity more absolute than it ever was in actuality, with – according to *my* version – truth and justice always proving themselves triumphant, but only just, against the clock and not a single second too soon.

In the studio I was normally a background figure, only required to be present for the sake of instant rewrites.

I enjoyed being with company after my solitary days above the Royal Mile. In the Spartan Café drinking Nessie's tea I would be in a kind of daze, taking nothing in of the goings-on around me and still imagining the dilemmas of my dramatis personae, especially those of the three principals – 'Guy Le Poitrel', 'Lady Jamesina', and 'Black Crawfurd'.

A couple of the older actors with bit parts in our epic made me feel less comfortable. One was an appalling bore, who would pretend to lower his voice whenever I walked in but who talked on – and on and on – in stage whispers, about the old glory-days of the Green Room. The carrot-wigged thesp who always seemed to be listening as she knitted – knitted unceasingly like Madame Defarge by the guillotine – was rumoured to be three-quarters deaf: even Miss McGillivray must have known of her disability, but we all persevered with the subterfuge of ignorance, treating her as a woman in full command of her aural faculties.

I felt that the Veterans resented my youth, and they would 'accidentally' call me by other names, those of my more illustrious predecessors in the drama department. Even their use of 'Mr Wardlaw' struck me as a calculated slight, since I was quite aware that I looked several years younger than my age, notwithstanding the fluffy attempt at a moustache which I sported.

Even more off-putting to me was the attention of Morag Scobie, who played 'Daft Grizel'. The casting seemed quite apt to me. Her thyroid eyes would stalk me round the studio or the canteen, but whenever I was within reasonable proximity she would shake out a newspaper and hold it up, or alternatively she bent forwards to consult her crossword clues, anything rather than have to speak to me. I guessed that she had listened to all the sly Green Room talk behind my back about when plays had *really* been plays, in that halcyon age, and that she was giving it her credence, although she was hardly old enough to know. She had a dished face, those too prominent eyes, and her mouth would drop open – as Daft Grizel's surely did too – every time Miss McGillivray barked out instructions.

The girl irritated me. She seemed so colourless, so vapid, an empty vessel waiting to be filled with a personality. And what was so abnormal about me that she could only stare and stare?

She had spoken to me once, and that was while I was waiting in the canteen for Dolores to return from the Ladies' Room. Miss McGillivray had followed Dolores inside, looking furious about something, perhaps about the amount of time she was giving to *me* and not to the script. Daft Grizel stopped by my table.

'Miss Scobie?' I said, hinting at my impatience.

'Mr Wardlaw – none of us is what you may think.'

I stared at her. It was my turn to be open-mouthed. What the hell was she talking about?

She coughed some grittiness out of her throat.

'It's – it's a strange life. Here. In this place.'

I shook my head.

'I'm sorry, I don't understand . . .'

'But that's just the point,' she said. 'Don't you see?'

She looked over her shoulder. Dolores was standing in the doorway, accepting a compliment from Douglas McWhinnie, aka 'Red-Rory Mauchlin' in the serial. McWhinnie imagined himself to be the flesh-and-blood ladykiller of our little band; I didn't doubt that the man's intentions were far from honourable ones, and I thought I could recognise a lustful eye when I saw one.

Daft Grizel vanished, and Dolores swanned across to my

[115]

table. To *our* table. She was a little pink in the face, but for me that only added to her allure. Her mouth was well-coated with lipstick, as if she had been standing for a long time in front of the mirror in the Ladies' – being politely harangued perhaps. Behind her the door from the corridor with its porthole window squeaked open and Miss McGillivray's voice rang out. As our leader called those with watches to synchronise them, preparing for count-down, she assiduously avoided looking in our direction.

Dolores sat down and pulled her chair closer to mine. I gawped at my arm in amazement. For the first time her hand was oh-so-casually resting on the crook of my elbow . . .

After that I kept thinking about the hand-hold, about what it might signify. My head was filled with a welter of possibilities. I had been steeling myself to offer some intimate gesture since the previous week, inspired all over again by noticing a new publicity photograph of Dolores lying on Miss McGillivray's desk at our script session three days before. Miss McGillivary had thrown it into a drawer when she saw me staring. Was Dolores threatening at last to leave us for television, which she had often told me was the exciting new place to be. 'Of course radio is a *craft*, darling, but we've all got to move with the times . . .'

That hand-hold, that hand-hold!

At last I got Dolores by herself.

'Would you,' I asked, 'would you please allow me to buy you a drink?'

'When, my love?'

'I – How about this evening?'

'*This* evening?'

She was picking back some fallen strands of hair with those exquisitely dainty long fingers.

'After – when we've – '

'I'm *so* sorry, Hamish, I'm going to be busy.'

'"Busy"?'

'I just can't, not tonight.'

'Oh well . . .'

'Lines,' she said, 'I'll be learning lines.'

'But,' I said, 'I haven't finished next week's – '

'No. No, of course not.' She flexed her smile, and dropped her hand to a point between neck and breasts. 'It's a television thing. Yes, really. Nothing may come of it, so don't hold your breath!'

'Oh.'

'I'm just – well, you know, reading it *through*.'

She offered me more apologies, but not on this occasion another hand-hold on my arm. I swallowed hard.

'Another time then?'

'Oh *yes*.'

Should I have suggested when? But the moment had gone before I could think to do so. She picked up her chinchilla jacket and threw it over her shoulders herself.

'Your umbrella – ' I said, retrieving it for her.

'Oh Hamish, bless you!'

Was it possible she would walk off 'Eagles' Crag', for the sake of something on that bastard invention television, which seemed to have turned her head, her lovely head?

She might have been reading exactly what was going through my mind.

'I do *love* doing this, you know,' she said. 'The scripts, they're so full of – well, life! Awfully good really . . .'

More smiles, publicity-still smiles just for me, and then she was off. To return home and learn her lines.

'Ciao, Hamish dear . . .'

Last out of the Green Room when Dolores was gone came Morag Scobie. Daft Grizel herself. Her mouth was hanging open, and her eyes were wide rounds, big as saucers. I cut her short, before she had a chance to start.

'I'm just off home.'

She nodded.

'Damned fine actress, Dolores,' I said, and I aimed the words straight at that imbecile face, so that she would know they were meant as a put-down to her.

She stared at me, just stared. She didn't reply. In her hand she was holding a newspaper. Another godawful crossword. Nothing would happen to her, her career wasn't going to take off, she would get nowhere: she summed up all the rest of them. Also-rans, *never*-rans. 'Good luck, Dolores,' I wanted to yell after my balletic muse. Radio was a craft only for those who knew how to appreciate it – like Dolores surely, in her heart of hearts.

Morag Scobie was preparing to speak, but I was tired after a long day of confinement in the stifling studio. I thought her shoulders heaved, as if she was vexed. Was I displeasing her *that* much? Very well . . .

'Look,' I said, 'I have to go.' The words came out sounding, oddly, gentler than I intended. 'You'll have to – you must excuse me . . .'

I picked up my briefcase and swung it under my arm. I really did want to get away. Today's hadn't been one of my more lucid scripts, with several abrupt cuts and unexplained jumps in the action and overall a wearied feel to the dialogue. Writing it, it had seemed quite all right and as per usual but something had been lost between that stage and our final transmission. A good deal of simple *sense* had been jettisoned by the time the continuity announcer embarked on the concluding credits. Craftsmen of course can be their own worst critics . . .

'Will you put out the lights?' I said.

'"The lights"?'

'Please.'

'Yes, but – '

'When you're going.'

Back to wherever it was, and I hoped – only a mite guiltily – that she sensed my rudeness in not enquiring where.

A few minutes later I found I had forgotten my script to take home with me, and I returned to the studio to look for it.

I pushed open the door into the outer room. It was in darkness. I was going to switch on the lights when I saw figures through the glass panel.

Miss McGillivray and Dolores.

I could hear them because the microphone had been left turned on. They were talking, very animatedly. About the script, I supposed, as I bent down in the gloom behind where I'd been sitting to search for my copy.

It *was* about the script, but not how I had first presumed.

'Why else,' Dolores was asking, hands on hips, 'why else do you imagine I keep on doing this bloody awful tosh?'

Miss McGillivray was staring up at her, but smiling.

'God, Dee, you're a beautiful creature when you're angry.'

'Jesus Christ!'

'But you *are* . . .'

'Where did you pick up lines like that?'

'It's a hazard of the job. It's contagious.'

[119]

'Why should I believe anything you say?'

'You believed me when I said "chinchilla jacket". Oh, ye of such little faith. Dee, thou ingrate – '

'No, I'm not. Lying little cow – '

'Call me what you will. It's all music to my ears, you lovely reprobate.'

Dolores stamped her foot. 'Why d'you only say these things when I'm like this? You never tell me – '

'Tell you what?'

' – that you love me. It makes me sick, it really does . . .'

Miss McGillivray laid her horny hand on Dolores' arm and moved closer, any more words were being sucked out of Dolores' throat into the upturned mouth of that smitten woman, but by that time I was in flight.

I stumbled out into the corridor.

I careered downstairs, unaware of where I was going.

The situation was trying to explain itself, to clarify, but I didn't want to focus on it, I just didn't want to think.

'Hamish!'

A woman's voice behind me caused me to stop on the landing. I spun my head round and looked back.

'Mr Wardlaw, I mean. I'm sorry – '

It was *her* again. That Scobie menace –

I blurted out, 'I have to – to get away – '

'To Edinburgh?'

' – get away from here. I don't – '

She nodded. Slowly, sadly. I narrowed my eyes to study her, something about . . . I was suddenly aware that her face was filled with, not the silly curiosity of before, but a strange and tender compassion.

I stood blinking up at her.

'I just wondered,' she said, 'when I saw you . . .'

I didn't move. My heart was still thundering in my chest.

'My aunty lives in Hillhead. Just up the road. I stay with her. We have our supper late on Thursdays.'

I started to shape words to speak, but no sounds would pass my lips.

'She listens to the programme, she's heard every one. She tells her friends what's happened if they have to miss it. She says it's just like history, it's so real. She says you must be terribly clever. I've told her, yes, you are, and – '

So . . .

So, I ended up in Hillhead, sitting between Morag and her Aunty Agnes, picking at the cold tongue and beetroot salad on my plate. The tenement flat was crowded with furniture and knick-knacks, decades' worth of over-buying, and it was so airless with the gas fire turned up full that I could hardly breathe. At her niece's prompting Miss Scobie produced a scrapbook: into its pages was pasted every Scottish newspaper notice that could ever have appeared about 'The Perils of Eagles' Crag' – more than I'd been aware of – about its cast and production team and its plots.

'You must be that proud of yourself,' Aunty Agnes said, and I didn't have the heart to tell the poor woman that I had inherited the job from someone better, who had quit after just a few weeks because he considered it such demeaning rubbish.

'It's awfu' popular, so it is.'

Morag smiled, to apologise for her aunt's unrefined accent. She had scarcely taken her eyes off me all evening. They were filled with devotion. How had I not noticed before? Now I understood the nature of the trap I had walked into, two floors up in hilly Hillhead, a trap tripped in a couple of seconds after months of preparation, with myself such an easy and nearly willing victim. Aunty Agnes pointed to a photograph of the script writer, of yours truly, that had appeared in the Glasgow *Bulletin*.

'That's our Morag's favourite picture of you. But it disnae do you justice, son, that's the truth. Right enough, Morag's always telling me that, so she is . . .'

Morag dropped her eyes momentarily, but surely not with embarrassment. As a formality rather, in this bizarre ritual of her and her aunt's contriving. She raised her eyes again almost immediately, to gloat upon me, to surrender no more than these few instants of her sweet triumph.

I missed the last train back to Edinburgh, but I found myself feeling quite sanguine about it.

I might have gone back to Hillhead. However I didn't. I decided I'd put up in a hotel, after I'd wandered about the streets for a while, those grids of fine Italianate buildings in Glasgow's centre.

The city proved to be all but deserted.

I did a circuit of the streets, so that I should come back to George Square eventually, and to the North British Hotel. I'd get a drink there, think of somewhere more modest to stay, or possibly even get a room in that august establishment and sod the expense.

I was hardly surprised when I saw them both emerging from the vestibule of the Central Hotel. It was one of Miss McGillivray's watering-holes, where she plied her male colleagues; that was how the gossip had started, that she must have a private income to support the extravagance of double-malts all round. The pair were carrying rolled umbrellas, just like businessmen. Out on Gordon Street, Dolores – tipsy and giggling – lifted hers and brandished it like a sword. Miss McGillivray responded in kind, and they swashbuckled for a few seconds, as I was always having my hero and his foes do. Dolores burst out laughing, and Miss McGillivray shook her head at them both, and then the pair strode off, ludicrously mismatched for height but intimately arm-in-arm and hip against thigh, just as cocky as Dumas's proud Musketeers.

I booked into a hotel for the night, a small and charmless apology for a hotel.

Lying awake on the saggy mattress I tried to remember what it was that Dolores and I had talked about during our intense exchanges in the canteen: that is, when she wasn't quizzing me on matters of radio technique.

About nothing very much, I was forced to conclude, finding it too hard to recall.

About the serial for one thing, and the direction in which I intended to take it. (Little did she know that it was the producer's privilege to decide.) About the weather, inevitably. And the new fashions in the newspaper: what did I think of those cropped bolero jackets from Paris? And about Miss McGillivray: how did I get on with her, was she easy to work with?

'Work *for*,' I had to correct her, and she stared at me quite blankly for a few seconds until it occurred to her to smile. 'Of course,' she said, 'of course, darling.'

I couldn't even remember now from my lumpy bed if she was good or not at her job, if the character she played – 'Lady Jamesina' – 'lifted from the page', as the term was amongst us radio hacks. Miss McGillivray had plucked her out of a long list of hopefuls for the job, rescuing her from the tundra-life of repertory theatre out in the sticks. A return to provincial rep. was still there as a persistent threat, a Damocles' sword held over that pretty head on its long lean neck, just as Dolores would continue to torture her Svengali with her naïve praise of television, with the fact of her youth and with her boasts about her 'adaptablity'.

Miss McGillivray ruled the roost at Queen Margaret Drive, she was as secure in her job as the bricks and mortar of Broadcasting House itself, but her girlfriend had breasts perky enough to catch the eye of any red-blooded managerial fellow (with or without wife at home) who was set up in a position to discuss the opportunities of the new medium with her, tête-à-tête and in some depth, at their mutual convenience.

I travelled back on the first train in the morning.

I decided somewhere between Lenzie and Falkirk that I'd had enough of my fantastic Covenanters and their juvenile japes.

Edinburgh loomed into sight, the first drops of rain spattered against the window glass, and I thought that it was altogether a different prospect seen in this half-light, quite grey and workaday. On the last stretch into Waverley Station I looked out through the engine smoke, up at the Castle on its bleak cliff, at the tall and grimy limpet buildings on the Mound, at the stepped corbie-stane roofs.

I was unaffected by the kitschness, and my mind was stilled.

Back up on the Royal Mile, I discovered a blocked drain in my galley kitchen. I let it be. Ensconced in the cramped Spartan, drinking Nessie's tea, I revived a little. I found I was drifting in and out of the conversations around me. I studied those faces. Two matronly assistants from a haberdashery shop, an undertaker, a couple of policemen, our milkman from the dairy, a few students, a brace of street-walkers taking the weight off their feet. Like Morag, they had been right here all this time, under my nose, and I had scarcely even noticed. They offered me a different kind of potential. Smaller stories, contemporary subject matter.

Tales of violence and romance, in tandem as they were in 'Eagles' Crag', but taking place in this truer world of reality we inhabit.

What I needed now was – somehow, by dint of hard effort – to find the voice that was my own. It would require me to sit patiently at my plain deal table, listening with the windows open to the life being lived out there on the streets, in the vennels and wynds: recording its pulse, and using my new and experimental voice to try to speak in many.

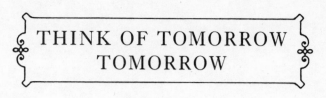

THINK OF TOMORROW TOMORROW

Juan Forn

translated by Norman Thomas di Giovanni
and Susan Ashe

Take therefore no thought for the morrow: for the morrow shall take thought for the things of itself. Sufficient unto the day *is* the evil thereof.

Matthew 6: 34

According to the notice-board, the plane was leaving at 18:42. It was after five o'clock, and the departure lounge was no longer the glass and moquette desert it had been at twenty-five past two, when she arrived, perspiring freely. She had got there early because she wanted to leave this dreadful city as fast as she could. Because she wanted to stop thinking that, barely three weeks earlier, one innocent June morning on that very spot, she had believed like a fool that a whole range of pleasant experiences lay before her while she learned precise, textbook English together with forty other boys and girls, all nineteen-year-old foreigners like herself.

She could no longer bear the way the tarmac in the road went soft in the sun, the sweetish smell of fried chicken, the cloying breath of men on the underground and in lifts, the over-intense stares of women in bars and cool museum rooms. She could no longer bear strangers sitting next to her in a dark cinema or passers-by brushing against her or bumping into her every time she walked along the street. She could no longer even bear the amiable faces of the other girls on the language course. She had spent the last day in her hotel room, with the television turned to the wall and on full blast to drown out the deafening noise of traffic. She had stayed in bed, curled up in a ball, every now and again wiping her face with a damp towel and ticking off the hours one by one until it was time to leave for the airport.

The air-conditioning in the lounge was almost soothing, as were the background music and the announcements in two languages of flights departing to and arriving from countries less hostile than this one. She was sitting in a row of seats with their backs to the automatic doors; this way, without their noticing her, she could see the passengers who came in. At about four o'clock she tried to pass the time by guessing who would be travelling on the same plane as she and where the rest might be going. But, with a touch of panic, she quickly gave up her little game when it struck her that others might be staring at her with equal curiosity. Was she ill? More than ill – she was unhinged. A generalised burning sensation, especially at the back of her neck and in her cheekbones, was melting her last reserves of self-control. If she were to remain in this country much longer, if she were not to have a drastic change of scene and see something familiar – her sister Marisa waiting for her at Ezeiza Airport, say – something terrible was going to happen to her.

Across from her, a couple dressed in shorts were kissing interminably. She stared at them for three or four seconds and suddenly got up. She had already checked her suitcase in but she refused to shed her silver-coloured knapsack, which was empty except for her passport, a bit of money, several cassettes, and a Walkman, which for the last hour or so had not helped at all.

There was background music in the toilets too. She saw herself in the mirror and decided she looked terrible. Pleasant experiences, she thought. With such a ridiculous round face, what else could you have? She was trying to make herself cynical. But it was no use. Seizing a little plastic Hermès envelope, she tore it open with her teeth and wiped her face with the cologne-drenched tissue. The refreshing sensation made her blink. She rested the knapsack on the marble counter, took a comb out of a tiny bag, and began mechanically to put on make-up, oblivious of the face that was emerging out of her tense, drawn features. Suddenly she stopped. Someone was singing – singing like a lunatic. Two women in floral dresses and enormous dark glasses gave her a sidelong glance. It's me. *I'm* singing, she thought, and a little laugh escaped from her. She glared at the women in the mirror. At once they stopped whispering and hastily left.

'Hags,' she said. 'Can't a person sing in a public place any more?' Before zipping up her pack, she looked in the mirror again. She tried to smile. She did not want to go on looking at herself.

When she got back to the lounge, someone had taken her seat and there wasn't a free one left. The couple in shorts were still kissing as if the end of the world were at hand. She strolled along past the windows of the duty-free shop; she bought some mint chewing gum to take the bad taste out of her mouth. She wandered through the half-empty shops until the sugary voice from the loudspeaker system announced her flight. Impossible, it was impossible. Either she had not heard the earlier announcements or something had swallowed up a chunk of time – the last fifteen minutes. The idea frightened her out of her wits, more even than the fact of missing her flight. Because the voice had just said, 'Last call for passengers boarding KLM Flight 367, with stopovers in Mexico City, Lima, and Buenos Aires.' Last call? What about the earlier calls? Were they trying to leave without her? Had there been no previous announcements on purpose?

She began to run to the departure gate. People gawked at her. She tried to compose herself, to walk in a civilised manner, but her legs were moving by themselves. The KLM official raised his eyebrows and gave her a perfectly silly smile as she rummaged in the knapsack for her boarding pass, but when he heard her first sob his face became solicitous and professional. It was a dry, tearless sob, almost out of place.

'Do you feel all right? Take it easy. There's no need to worry.'

'I'm not worried,' she said through clenched teeth, and she had to stop herself adding, You thought I wasn't going to notice that the plane was leaving, when she almost tore from the depths of the knapsack her heaven-sent orange boarding pass.

'Have a pleasant trip. Thank you for choosing KLM,' said the bright face of the official. She didn't reply. She entered the absurd tube that connected the lounge with the plane, ignored the stewardess's welcoming smile, and reached her seat out of breath. Window. Luckily a window seat. And luckily, she also thought, she could not see the jet engine behind the clear double plastic oval window. She dropped into the seat, leaned back, sighed, shut her eyes. She was perspiring again. She was trembling again. Once more she felt unable to open her eyes.

'Excuse me. You are sitting in my place, I think,' said the voice of an angel. For what the girl heard was not altogether a human voice. Lightly feminine, yes, but neither a woman's voice nor of this world.

The girl opened her eyes and saw a smile. Beside the smile waved a ticket with a seat number on it. Around the smile was a radiant face, a very young face, framed by a wimple. *Wimple* – is that what it's called? the girl wondered. She also returned the smile. Before saying anything, she smiled stupidly. Then she heard herself say, 'What? What did you say?'

'You are in 27W – my seat,' said the nun, her voice level and unrushed, in perfect English.

'Yes, of course, I must have made a mistake. I'm so scatterbrained. Then that's my place,' the girl said, trying to move from the window seat to the one next to it. Somehow the manoeuvre became fraught with complication. She kept tossing her head back to get the hair out of her face, while at the same time attempting to disentangle herself from the Walkman's leads, the straps of her knapsack, and her seat belt. She felt frantic, helpless, and a stream of obscenities stuck in her throat.

The nun's hand lay on her arm. 'It's all right. Don't bother, really. We can always change later.' Still resplendent, she absorbed and gave off again all the light that came in through the window.

The girl slumped back into her seat – which was not hers – and the knapsack slipped out of her hands.

'Thanks,' she said. And with a final effort she managed to fasten her seat belt. She shut her eyes as something like tears, something less dry and abrupt than the sobs that had been escaping from her every now and then over the last few days, could not be suppressed. She did not open them again until the plane levelled out and she heard the other passengers unbuckling their belts.

When the stewardesses began to hand out the meal trays, the girl dared look straight at her neighbour for the first time. The nun's habit was pearl grey. As was her wimple, under which was a skull cap that covered her ears. She was very young, she was absurdly beautiful. Why a nun, then? the girl wondered, furtively staring at the perfect oval of her companion's face and her sparkling eyes, with their green tinge. And her nose – the kind of nose the girl had always wanted, small and at the same time firm, a nose that distinguishes a perfect face from one that is merely beautiful.

The nun was answering the stewardess with the drinks trolley. Water, she was saying. Not iced or even cold; just water. The girl asked for Coca-Cola, which seemed flat and more metallic-tasting than usual, and she left most of her meal untouched.

After that, evening fell. And maybe because of the reddish glow, maybe because of the music from her Walkman (Calamaro's voice crooning, 'Sometimes I wonder if we'll part; you say you'll never break my heart'), maybe because of the unreal dimness in the plane, for a while she could forget the ethereal closeness of the nun and her own anguished existence, which was dammed up in all her pores. But when the cassette ended, and the flame of the sky turned purple and then black, and she leaned down to slip off her shoes, hoping that the relief would start at her feet and climb to her knotted breast, she thought she would choke.

Could a person literally choke over something like that, something one *saw*? First there were the nun's Franciscan sandals, their soft leather stained with use; then her feet, encased in white stockings that must have been plain, that could not have been silk, but that nevertheless appeared to be of a mesh that did not exist in this world. At rest, side by side and slightly inclined to suit the angle of her legs, the feet set off in the girl a sudden, paralysing spasm. My goodness, they're only feet, she thought. What's happening to me. But the effect was hypnotic; in spite of the deafening throb in her temples, the girl simply could not straighten up. Nor could she take her eyes off the nun's feet. Her hands, which seemed full of sand, took on a life of their own and reached down, while the girl's face sank lower and lower, until she was caressing and cradling the nun's foot that was slightly off the floor, her right foot, which rested almost weightlessly on the left instep, the foot that the girl held and pressed to her face. Then a gigantic sob rose in her throat and she let it burst out.

She did not know if she had made a sound. She was not

thinking about anything. She was barely able to control her feelings, one in particular. Because somehow she knew that the foot could take away everything that was eating at her inside.

When the nun's hands gently lifted her, the girl allowed herself to be raised, first by the shoulders, then (and even more gently) by the head. She saw only a black sea surrounding a bright oval that whispered a comforting singsong in a harsh language, staccato, musical. The hands laid her against the seat back but kept caressing her hair, her cheeks, drying her first tears. When the girl managed to control her sobs – or at least when they were less fitful – she opened her eyes and said, 'I don't know . . . I don't know what happened. Please forgive me.' And she added, absurdly, 'Can I speak to you in Spanish? Do you understand Spanish?'

'Yes. *Un poco yo comprendo,*' said the nun's voice in a Spanish that contained more vowels than consonants.

The girl placed her hand on the hand that was smoothing her hair.

'Did I do wrong?' she said. 'I meant no . . .'

Still looking at her, the nun put a handkerchief into the girl's fingers. Then the nun closed them and held them firm.

'When it passes, you can talk if you want to.'

The girl closed her eyes. She thought everything was going to begin again, but it passed. She gulped air noisily and suddenly she felt absolute calm. She opened her eyes. She turned her head without lifting it from the seat.

'I couldn't stay there another minute. That city . . . is horrible. I didn't know – when I arrived I didn't know – I didn't think that . . . I'm sorry,' she said abruptly, 'but I can't call you sister.'

'Call me Gretchen,' said the perfect, radiant face.

[135]

'Gretchen,' the girl said, 'why is it so frightening? Is it the same for you nuns? I'm not, I'm not . . . like that. I've never hurt a soul. Why are they all so cruel, why are they all so . . . so vicious and depraved?'

She had almost spat out the last words, in spite of the fact that she spoke effortlessly, without moving her lips. The nun gave her a questioning look.

'What do you mean by that?'

'How old are you, Gretchen?'

'Twenty-six,' said the nun, enunciating each syllable unblinkingly, but for the first time slightly put out. 'And you?'

'Nineteen,' the girl said almost inaudibly. 'Or nineteen million – I don't know any more.'

'What are you talking about? Tell me, please.'

'I don't know. About myself, about what I am. About what I might have been, do you understand? Because I never chose. I thought one always had a choice. I don't know, I just don't know. Is it too late now? Am I going to be this all my life, then? Nothing more than this?'

The nun caressed the girl's hand and gave it a little pat.

'So, this is why you are crying? Because you are a pretty young lady?'

Then the girl began to cry – silently, unable even to shut her eyes.

'It is all right, what you are saying. Soon a time will come when everything will be simpler for you.'

The girl shook her head. She raised her hand, covered her mouth with the handkerchief, and said in a choked voice, 'No, no, no. It's something else. It's not an adolescent problem. It's a lot more complicated. Don't you see?'

That was when the girl realised that the nun did not understand, that she understood nothing about anything. It was ridiculous. It was even funny that Gretchen should be trying to understand anything in her unsure, faltering Spanish, and that the girl was struggling to explain. Explain what? She had been caressing a nun's foot and now she was trying to explain to the nun how irreversibly screwed up her life was, for specific but perhaps not very obvious reasons. Yes, it was even funny. Not to say appalling.

'It's all right, Gretchen. What does it matter? What can you do, anyway?' The girl chose not to go on looking at the perfect, puzzled face. She was afraid of seeing the nun become less attractive at this rejection and of having to feel guilty about that too. The girl let her hair fall over her face and she twisted the damp handkerchief. What was going to happen now? I don't care, she thought. I don't care about anything any more. Let her think what she likes and leave me in peace.

But Gretchen had something to say. The girl heard her wetting her lips; she even thought she heard her searching for the words before saying, 'You are confused, I think. Are you listening? But that is not so bad. Something now I remember they say in my country – take one day at a time. This is correct in Spanish, *ja*?'

Gretchen's words fell into order only after they had entered the girl's head. Maybe she really had heard the nun searching for the words, because now the girl heard them fitting one behind the other until she understood the full sense that Gretchen intended.

'Yes,' the girl said. 'That's correct.' And she felt that her face was stretching very slowly in an expression like a smile, an expression that had nothing bad in it. Nothing bad. Because she knew the saying, and even who had said it; she was an addict of the person who had said it now and for always. 'Are you sure it's a saying from your country? I could swear it's something Scarlett says at the end of *Gone with the Wind*.'

For a second or two, Gretchen's smile remained fixed. Just as it began to look false she spread the smile across her whole face, giving it back its earlier luminous beauty.

'Oh, good. Because for me Spanish is so hard, still.' She sighed, satisfied, passing over the name Scarlett O'Hara with complete naturalness. 'Try to sleep now, yes? And, when you wake up, yesterday is farther away and you can think better.'

She put the little pillow behind the girl's head and brushed the hair out of her eyes. And she did something else too – something that had a lot more to do with her age than with her status as a nun and her Heavenly Lord. She put the earphones on the girl and plugged in the Walkman.

A little while later, in a pause between one song and the next, the girl opened her eyes slightly and sneaked a look to her left. The lights in the plane were out, and the drone of the engines was almost inaudible. She knew she was going to fall asleep at any moment and she was already a little groggy, but anyway she sneaked a look to her left. In the dark, her seat upright, Gretchen was watching the screen several rows forward. She sat erect, very serious, and with that kindly bewilderment that seemed the hallmark of her expression. The film had no subtitles; it was *Rocky*, or one of its sequels. The girl laid her head back and let her eyes close again. She tried to picture some future soul, lost and confused, bumping into Gretchen and being consoled with the words of Sylvester Stallone; the girl tried to picture how many would-be German sayings Gretchen had disseminated over the world on her mission of salvation. But the girl's weariness and Calamaro's voice on the Walkman were carrying her slowly and gently off to the probable country of dreams, and, without the slightest resistance, she let herself be borne away.

LOVE MARKS

Philip MacCann

Every second Sunday, all through that autumn of musk-scented rain and those yellow shadows you might have noticed, I was catching an afternoon coach into London to see a child. Oh, it was so pointless from the start. He needed a real mother, not a crazy woman like me. We had to meet on Mare Street Hackney in the queue for my bus, making out we were strangers. Can you believe that? Every second Sunday was the same. Until, as the New Year approached, it came to an end. And then spring bounced in very sensible and positive-minded. I could nearly hear the birds beginning to cheep, 'Let him be, Jacqueline.' Well, those little conservatives would have been right, of course. I never doubted that.

One morning I'd got up feeling panicky. I'd been thinking how little I had so far and all that. I'd only recently stopped sleeping with a woman. We'd both been trying hard to make do with it. When each of us realised the other knew we could hardly look each other in the eye. Most of the people I knew were nicely into a rut by then and it seemed I was the oldest of them at thirty-five. I decided that day to go to London since it was one of the days I didn't work. To take my mind off things. But I just seemed to dangle there feeling left out and slightly weird. All the housewives were out with their babies and squeaky-clean kids in cute new uniforms. There was a strong moon in the sky. Later I happened to run into a young Cockney girl outside a shoe shop near the Angel – she'd been into me at a time when I'd been more into trying to be normal. Twice

when I'd met her she was with a wild-looking homeless kid
who was very often filthy; we'd go into a snack bar for ice-
cream and argue politics. I wasn't even all that fond of her
– she tried to dye her hair Irish, did herself up like a
marigold, looked just as dumb as men would say she was,
you know the type. That day I had a nice tweed jacket and
tie on and I couldn't help feeling conspicuous in her
presence: you could tell there was this class gulf between
us, I had an appalling job and she had nothing. The top of
the boy's left training shoe was ripped off. Just to be
predictable or to avoid a shower we went to a snack bar
again that day. But she was in a crap mood. Oddly, I
thought her hands were too big for her body like a woman
badly painted. My optimism was so fragile it was about to
shatter on one of her harder words, everything was disinc-
lined that day. Including the ice-cream. Death by Chocolate? It didn't even sting. And she was pissed off at
Robbie. Which was unfair, he had problems. Soon a dispute
developed. 'I'm not getting meself in trouble over you,' she
hissed at him. He frowned at his dish. Basically she
wouldn't put him up because the police were looking for
him. I didn't really know the facts but I didn't support her.
I didn't say anything, I just kept dipping my finger in the
ice-cream and feeling unreasonable for doing it. He was
breathing audibly. At last she stood up, reassured us how
little anything meant to her anyway and flapped out. He
blinked away light in his eyes. He was quite tough-looking,
about thirteen. He wore a little ink spot on his cheek. I
handed him a Kleenex. 'In case you want to blow your
nose,' I said. I bought him another ice-cream and said
everything would turn out good. I bet everyone in the snack
bar thought I was coaxing him to be gay or something. We
got up and went on to the street. 'Well . . .' I plucked a
tenner out of my pocket. 'Take this.'

[142]

'Nice one,' he said. And he winked at me.

I'll be honest. Once or twice I'd actually daydreamed about snatching this boy away, looking after him. After that wink I just wanted to throw my arms around him. But then I thought: maybe not such a good idea. I'd just do it in a really strange way. And he was probably breaking some law just dressed like that. He looked cold. I asked what he was going to do. He didn't answer.

'Why won't you go back to your gran?'

'They'll catch me, that's all.' He scratched his tooth.

I took a bus into the West End. On it I had another of my little maternity crises, but I rationalised it quite well. I went into a few shops. Later I caught my coach back to Ipswich. Obviously he'd be all right, I told myself, he'd been all right before me. As the coach was driving through Leytonstone I suddenly surprised myself. I stood up. I walked up to the driver. I asked him to let me off somewhere near. Miserable and soaked and with almost no idea what I was doing, I rang a friend from the High Road. I told her I wasn't needed at the market in the morning, asked her could I stay the night. I took a taxi to her flat. Then as we were blowing on hot chocolate I happened to say, 'You know, I'd live in London if the rent wasn't so dear.' 'You could always live in squalor in Hackney,' she said, 'like Emma.' 'Emma?' I remembered her. I always thought she was incredibly unusual in that, sexually, she was exactly the norm. According to my friend she'd just flitted from a room.

The next day I walked around Hackney with an A-Z searching for Navarino Road. The old bricks showed up sharp in the drenched light. There were some bags stuffed with bones on the footpath. It was a long road with wide shrivelled trees and more crinkled leaves than air. Beside a takeaway there was a junk shop selling some stupid paintings, most of a skeleton, putrid flowers in the original

gruesome vase, perhaps you know it. I made out the house,
73 or 75, I think. Outside it there were green and mustard
rusty cars parked bumper to bumper, a cement mixer, a
white mini. I liked it on the outside. I knocked. The day's
wrinkles were also on the landlord's wife. And she was
wearing an insulting daffodil cardigan, you had to take it
personally. It told me everything about her, she was a bit
like my aunt, one of those women who really never wanted
anything else. She showed me the bedsit. Little corner
room on the top floor, walls like cardboard, damp patches
on them, a view of gnawed chimney stacks, skylights,
aerials. Don't ask me what I was at. I took it. Then I went
to the Marigold, told her I could take the boy somewhere
next Sunday if he was still on the run. I went home on the
coach feeling infertile or left out or like a serial killer, I
don't know what. On Sunday morning I returned with a
small suitcase. I plugged a kettle in, set two cups out, some
plates and cutlery, a toaster, bunged the suitcase in the
filthy wardrobe that blocked half the window. And it was
up to this high secret square of dusk and chimney smoke
and clouds the colour of bruises, that I suppose you'd have
to say I smuggled Robbie. At the calmest time of the week.
A disappointing total of nine times. Nine times in those
four strange months. I remember them so well. When every
brown morning was dripped on by greasy nights. And
soggy twilight began at noon.

The first time I was to meet him I didn't think there was
any point. How could I be his mother? He was squatting
with some older boys close by in Bethnal Green. I could
get off my coach in Hackney so I'd told the Marigold I
would meet him there at the bus stop for my bedsit at four
o'clock. I turned up. I stood under the scaffolding on sand
grinning at the thought of myself and waiting for this

neglected figure to appear behind craquelure of rain. I'd
tried to dress down as well as I could. Just for the sake of
that ever-frowning unblinking peeping police eye. Pres-
ently, I noticed he was in the queue. We didn't speak. He
had no jacket, a lace was missing from his shoe – I'd never
be able to look normal beside him. At last the bus arrived.
We boarded. It was stupid, I sat on a separate seat. A squad
car passed us. I just knew this had to be illegal. Near
Navarino Road we got off. We smiled at each other. 'We'll
need milk,' I said quietly.

'Get us a Coke.'

'You stay outside.'

'Coke.'

I nipped into a corner shop. A doubled-up, knotted
woman greeted me with what actually looked like approval.
It was amazing she was still on her feet. She was even more
elderly and yellow than her window display cornflakes. I
bought some inessentials: bread, ham, fags for him, milk,
one packet of crisps, a lighter, one tin of Coke, playing
cards, a tomato in case. When I came out of the shop again
he was across the street scrounging a fag from a guy in a
waxy jacket. I was almost going to walk away. I passed
them, ignoring him, until he ran up to my side: 'Have you
got that can?' His Cockney features were free like a berserk
mechanism. I had the casual face of a ventriloquist as we
walked. I asked, 'Did he approach you?' Well, I was anxious
for him. 'Wha' d'you mean, approach?' He slurped. There
was a smell of fireworks or spookiness, or was it just
Hackney? I kept asking myself: what do you think you're
at? Coughed mist, twinkling shards of bottles, inky figures
on the walls and roads. We both peeked in as we passed the
junk shop. Grinning fish. A hairbrush on a claw. I couldn't
believe any of it. Already starlight licked about the bins.

[145]

We came to the house. I lifted open the narrow gate. 'Quiet going in, Robbie.' High above the rooftops, three, four times higher, a newspaper was flapping.

We scaled the stairs and I noted how top-floor bedsits were especially inconvenient to the smuggler. At last, with a flexed face, I opened the deadlock and let him in ahead of me. I locked it from the inside, tried it. There was a smell. 'Sorry about this room, it's horrible, isn't it?' There was only the gross wardrobe that took up about an eighth of the room, one clapped-out oven on wheels, a few other things, bedside table and lamp, and the broad low bed that had probably known everyone and everything. He sat on it. I threw off my coat, wiped my hair on a blanket. 'Dry your hair with this.' Then I boiled the kettle, I needed coffee. 'So.' He ripped open his crisps. I took my cup, scooped out the blue milk from the week before. 'Tell me.'

'Wha'?'

'About yourself.'

'Wha' about meself?'

I brought two coffees over. I sat on the soily carpet. There was a silence. I took a sip. I heard him breathe in. 'Talk,' I said. I lifted the pack of cards.

'Wha' about?'

I took the cards out. I couldn't think what to say. I shuffled them, pretending to concentrate. 'Just talk,' I said softly. I looked at him.

'Just talk, please, talk,' he sighed and munched. I must have looked hurt because he added, 'Nah, I'm only messing.'

'Play cards,' I suggested with a croaky voice. He slipped on to the carpet. He dealt them. His clothes were pungent. He tore up the jokers, saying they were unlucky. We began to play. Gradually a darkness crept over us, aubergine in colour. I didn't know what game we were playing. He just

picked and flicked down cards capriciously. Underneath us
someone came in. You know what this boy reminded me
of? It sounds pathetic, but I was thinking of those sentimen-
tal pictures that cluttered up the market where I helped
out. Sometimes Robbie had one of those quite overdrawn
innocent pouts, very misleading. I could see him curled up
in a filthy shadow with mud under his fingernails. I tried to
think of something to say. 'You know . . .' I smiled at him.
'I haven't even said hello to you yet.'

'Hello.'

'How's it going, for God's sake?'

'It's going and it's going and it's gone.' I smiled at that.
And then he added, 'For God's sake.' Noises sounded from
underneath us.

'Tell me.' I spoke low. 'Can't you go back to the home?'
He shrugged. He kicked his trainers off and sat in the most
world-weary socks. 'You can't stay on the run.'

'What's it to you?'

I looked seriously. 'I care,' I told him.

Now his eyes were on mine. He kept them on me as he
asked, 'Why did you take me here?'

My heart quickened. I set down my cards. He wasn't
smiling.

'Wha' d'you want me for?'

I made a laugh. 'I just thought . . .' I began. I didn't
know what to say. I thought: okay, it's a big mistake, I
don't know what I'm doing. At that moment I felt I heard
something in the flat below. A loud wince. 'What's going on
there?' I said. We listened. It was quiet. I eased on to my
feet. I leaned by the window. It was sellotaped and bloomed
olive. It sounded like birds were trilling outside. We looked
at each other's faces. I lowered the venetian blind and
switched the lamp on. He lit a fag. I crouched down again.
His face was thinking about the silence. We held it and

[147]

smiled at each other. We were waiting for another wince. He bit his lip. A moment later what happened? No, there was no noise. We simply burst out giggling together. I don't know why. We were giggling at the whole situation in this ridiculous room, I suppose. At length I stood up again. 'Will you eat something?' I asked. He nodded shyly.

I made elaborate sandwiches; we didn't listen for any more ejaculations below. As he ate he showed me a card trick. I hardly followed it because my eyes were on him. I watched the tiny trapeze of his features, consonants exploding. And then suddenly I realised I was touching his shoulder. I got up and moved. 'You see if you were ever found in here, Robbie?' I whispered as he shuffled. He raised his eyebrows, opened his bready mouth. 'You know I'm not trying to put ideas in your head.'

'Wha' ideas?'

'I mean you're free to do what you want.'

'Pick a card,' he said. 'Wha' is it?'

I took one, tutting to myself. 'Knave of Spades.'

He concentrated with his eyes closed. 'Is it the Knave of Spades?'

I showed him an apologetic face. 'No, it's not.' We grinned at each other.

'Then it must be the King of, wha' d'you call them, flowers. Right?'

'How did you know that?'

'Ah, the appliance of science.'

Over the next two weeks I couldn't help pretending I was a mother. I had a dream that the two of us were playing in a park in the sun. How wonderful it would be to be able to agree with society and be conventional, I realised. Then the next Sunday I was with Robbie we were leaning on the bed among only light and dark and smoke. And I asked, 'What would happen if the landlord knocked?' The shadows took possession of our bodies. 'I suppose you'd get locked up.' Gloom seduced him. 'I bet I'd be interrogated like hell.'

'I'll hide,' he mumbled. 'In that wardrobe.' We looked over at it, a patch of darker black.

'Could you?

There was a silence. He shrugged. 'Or if you like I could always kill meself.' He took out his lighter.

'That's not funny,' I snapped.

'Why don't I burn meself?' He tried to flick it on.

'Stop it.'

'Why!' He frowned. He flicked again. 'You don't give a toss.'

I listened below and made a gesture to speak more quietly. I sat up straight. 'Can we change the subject, please?'

'I'll kill meself one day,' he assured me. A bright flame shot above his fist.

I stood up. 'Well.' I swallowed and smiled. 'I don't know,' I said, 'about you . . .' I switched on the light. 'But I think it's gloomy in here.' I closed the blind. He didn't say anything more. I stood at the sink. 'What about one of my specials?' He ignored me. I put my hand on a loaf of bread. 'No?' He was just staring at the lighter. So I sat beside him. I asked was he hungry. He didn't say anything. 'You won't,' I said, I cleared my voice, 'kill yourself.' He was still staring. Poor Robbie. Somebody else might have put their arm around him right then. What a nice idea. But I knew it wasn't right to confuse him. I wanted him to be normal. I mean, God forbid he should turn out like me. I looked down at his hand. It was mucky. 'Things'll get better,' I said. He didn't respond. His fingers twitched. From somewhere in the house an alarm clock went off. 'Can I ask you something?'

'Wha'?'

'Would you show me your hand?'

'Wha?'

'Not to touch it,' I explained. 'Just show me.'

'There,' he laughed. It was scratched.

'Well,' I said. I pointed at his palm. 'I bet you're going to fall for a lovely girl soon.'

He looked at me with his mouth open. 'Why?'

'It's in your palm.'

His face followed a thought. 'Is it?' The corner of his lip twitched. 'Can you see if she'll give me a blow-job?' He examined his own palm. He made little expressions. Like dreams. They were like dreams bothered by dust squalls. 'That's all,' he said. 'I don't want nothing more.' I thought: charming! Even so-called innocence is caught up in the damage and filth, that male stuff. But who knows, maybe he was happy that way. He was scratching the pillow with his finger. 'D'you like it?' he asked quietly.

'Like what?' I said.

'Wha'?'

I wasn't following him. 'This?' I made a scratching gesture.

'Your hand?'

I laughed. 'What do you mean?'

'That's right, mush.'

'Is it?'

'Yeah,' he nodded truthfully, 'Tuesdays and Fridays.' He licked his knuckle.

Sometimes communication was great. One evening he began to speak about himself. We could hardly see each other in the room. London breathed at the window. He told me his earliest memories of being raised in a place called The Basin by his gran. It sounded almost exciting so long as I didn't have to live there. Outside toilets. A litter of kids. He loved telling it. An infancy haunted by ancient personalities the family couldn't forget. Some of what he said I couldn't even make out, to be honest. I listened to a syllable stream. To reed music. I understood that an uncle died, a child died and his indefatigable old gran proffered humorous wisdom. Never take advice from no one, she'd told Robbie – especially from me.

I mentioned my plain childhood growing up fairly hap-pily in, it wasn't even worth talking about, I said. 'Where?' – he pummelled me. Of all places, I told him, Nottingham, the centre of nothing. Home of Sweetex. I got him laugh-ing. My folks were all right, I confessed. I couldn't blame them, they were simple, straight. My dad was genuinely sad for me. And now, I suppose, I was feeling sad for this boy. In fact, I was beginning to feel protective – and I didn't like that. I could understand the concerns of those old judges with faces like withered bollocks. We were silent for a moment. Then he spoke.

'We could live here.' I didn't answer. He tapped my leg. 'The both of us.' I looked away. 'Jackie.' I stood up.

'What?'

It was so embarrassing.

'Can we?'

'No,' I said. 'It wouldn't be safe.' He pulled his lip. 'You'd attract attention.'

'I won't.'

He wasn't serious, it was only talk. 'You're just using me, aren't you?' I teased him.

'You're using me.'

'How?'

'I know wha' you're like.' He frowned at the wall.

Off and on I thought about buying things to civilise the room, as my dad would have put it; I had in mind something from that junk shop on Navarino Road, maybe a combusted pistol or a stuffed head. One dry Sunday evening I looked in the window when I was killing some time by walking to Mare Street for the coach after Robbie had got the bus. There was a framed photograph propped on the ground that seemed to have Robbie's London eyes. But then I was beginning to see Robbie everywhere, in babies, I saw an old woman once who looked like Robbie. There was also a deformed embryo. There were tentacles that inflated, and a lot of depressing stuff – a pair of glasses, rusty scissors. The worst thing of all I spotted was a joke finger. The shop probably had one of everything, I suppose we both could have learned about the whole world in there. Anyway, I couldn't think of anything to get that would be an improvement. But I knew it wasn't good taking Robbie into that stark room.

We sat around one Sunday frustrated by this and by the empty afternoon.

'Jackie,' he whispered.

'Yeah?'

'Hi.'

Our own responses exasperated us as well every time he farted and I protested. I'd only just got used to his unwashed smell. 'If we could go places together,' I said. 'Safely. I hate this room.'

'It's a cool flat,' he said. 'Stick up posters.' Muddy rain began smacking on the slates.

We started to play a ridiculous game. He stuck his finger in my ear. I lifted my elbow. He grinned. I put it in his mouth. Suddenly, he positioned his face close to mine. 'What're you doing?' I said. I could smell his hair. He was trying to bite my eyelashes. Well, I thought, that's different.

When he sat down again all I could think of saying was, 'Can you do this?' and I tied my fingers in a knot. He gave a baffled sneer. He stiffened his thumb. It bent really far back, he must have been double-jointed. 'You've a weird-looking thumb,' I said. It was damp. He pulled a bored face. 'How do you do that?' It just wasn't like a real one, it belonged in that junk shop. But then, I didn't care. God, why wasn't he my child. 'I'm under your thumb,' I said.

'Wha' d'you mean?'

'Certainly.'

'Wha'?'

'Thumb.'

'Why?'

'Because it's just so Yin, darling.' That was the sort of thing I did with Robbie, discovered the obvious.

We kept on joking. My idea was his thumb was the odd one out, the eccentric member of a category. The banana among fruit. The joker in the pack. 'Electric chair,' I suggested. 'Is dildo one?' he asked. We got sucked into this game, half-knowing what we were doing. Maybe it wasn't a real finger at all, we thought, maybe it belonged to its own group which included such oddities as: kidney bowls, 50p pieces, witches' hats, worm cake, suits of armour, cuckoo clocks, flying fish, pinking scissors. But his freak thumb had to be the nicest.

'D'you want that?' he asked and he showed me the ring on his finger.

I looked at it. 'Well, I'll be honest, no.'

'How much would you give me for it?' I shook my head. 'Take it.'

'No.'

'It's yours.'

I touched the ring. 'It's too small,' I told him.

[153]

'Pull it,' he told me.

'No.'

'Here,' he said, 'it's not my dick you're pulling.'

'It won't come off!' I shouted. And that was exactly when someone underneath us made a noise again.

I shushed him. We listened. The traffic hissed below. Robbie scratched his eye. Then I thought I heard something else. And it sounded like a slap.

I screwed up my face to listen, but Robbie spoke. 'So am I staying here or what?' He hadn't heard it. He was scrutinising the walls.

'Listen.' There was nothing to hear now. 'What's going on down there?'

'I'm staying? Nice one.' I sat and thought. 'Unless you don't trust me.'

'I don't like the sound of that,' I whispered. The house was quiet.

'D'you not like this room? I'll do something to it.'

'Be quiet a minute, I'm trying to listen,' I said. But he swung off the bed. He walked up to the door. He said sharply:

'Let me out!'

He was tugging the door. 'What're you doing?' I said. But he yelled:

'Just let me out!'

I shot towards him. 'Robbie, I . . .' I didn't know what to say, I didn't want to inflame him. He was staring at the lock. Then underneath us there began a succession of slaps. I pretended I didn't hear anything and said, 'What is it?' But my voice was cracked.

'What am I doing here?' he mumbled.

'I'm not keeping you here,' I said kindly. I unlocked the door. 'If you want to go you can.'

He shrugged. 'You don't want me here.'

'I do.'

He hesitated. 'Can I stay then?'

I locked the door again. 'Make up your mind.' He slouched to the bed and perched on it lighting a fag. He inhaled smoke. I didn't speak. Simply for something to do and until he calmed down, I made toast. I stood by the window. I didn't even eat it. I made out the subdued roof and dour windows of what just had to be a court house standing before a vast spare ground. I didn't know what I thought about this whole situation, to be honest. I was really very divided. I suppose it was only right for me to tell him after a long silence: 'I shouldn't be seeing you at all.' He looked at his trainers. 'I'm not good for you.'

'Why?'

'I'm weird, for God's sake.' He tore at a trainer. 'I'm influencing you.' Outside above a smashed dormer window somebody had left a lunch box and some electricity cable. 'D'you think,' I asked him, 'I'm doing you damage?'

He snapped, 'Wha' d'you mean? Like cruel?'

'Yeah,' I hushed him. 'Am I?' He didn't answer. After a moment I spoke again. 'Am I?' Again he said nothing. 'Robbie?' He swallowed. I thought he was about to speak. But he got to his feet. He let out a shriek. Under his wrist he was holding a flame.

Immediately I grabbed his hand. He was groaning at the top of his voice. He dropped to his knees. 'You're okay, Robbie,' I stammered. I tried to get my hand over his mouth. He rocked back and forward now. He thumped his head with his fist. I tried to stop him. I could hear talking somewhere in the house. 'Robbie, please be quiet,' I said. 'Everything's okay, I promise.' He buried his face in the carpet. I just couldn't calm him. He kept on groaning loud. I stood up. I didn't know what to do. I almost felt like laughing. I walked up and down the room while he wailed.

[155]

'Robbie, please stop crying,' I begged. 'The police'll be here in a minute.' It wasn't any use. I just didn't know what to do. I tried getting down beside him again. 'Everything'll be all right,' I promised him.

Over time he became quieter. Nobody bothered us from the other flats. At last when he seemed to relax a bit I whispered, 'What is it?' He sniffed. 'You can tell me.' His ear was dirty. 'Is there something I don't know?'

At last he spoke. 'They make you do things in that home,' he said.

I gazed at him. I had to clear my mind. 'What do you mean?' He didn't answer. 'Who makes you?' I flustered.

'Wha'?'

'What do you do?' He raised his eyebrows. 'Robbie?'

He mumbled, 'Things.'

'What things?'

'Different things.'

If only I could have shown him how much I cared. I brought my face closer to his. 'What kind of things?' I whispered.

He shrugged. 'Clean the windows and all,' he said.

I made something for him to eat. My legs were juddering from all the fuss. Well, a very convincing thought came into my mind now. It was just the sort of malcontentment that suited our oppressors so well, and here I was thinking it. I was thinking how perverse Nature was. Here was a young boy, beautiful on the outside, in hell on the inside. But it didn't matter to Nature what any of us felt, we were just meant to look good. All the injustice and hardship of a person's life, the smell of their poverty, their broken thumbs – we had to love it, the surface expressed it in a really delightful way. God, I thought, what a false world it is. Not a very good effort at all.

When we were sharing my coffee he asked me a question.

I'd been waiting for it. 'Have you never done it with a bloke, Jackie?' But I couldn't focus on this now. To be honest, I was jumpy from every creak I heard downstairs. I wanted to think. I could see so clearly how bad his life was, but had I brought him into something much worse? 'How d'you do it with another girl?' I looked around the room pretending not to have heard. In a while he daydreamed as he sat. Me, I couldn't stop thinking. I was picturing some weird waxy man who might live below, a mockery of fatherhood. He could offer you the plump hand of love that loved to slap. I thought about him, and about all the discreet ululation, disabusal, finger-licking, the zooerastia and general bonking going on in Hackney houses. And, in the whole of London, the psychic life glimmering in all those bricks. I shuddered at what might lie around Robbie every day. I'd seen plenty of details. I'd encountered the arses that loved eggs. And everyone I knew had said the same thing: there was every flaw imaginable. Somewhere there would be spinsters scolding their mirrors, some psycho contemplating angels. We both sat back on the bed in silence. I don't know what he was thinking, but I let myself imagine a sumptuous young lady, black-clad as a governess, whose sole yearning was just to drift down to Pimlico chimneys on an umbrella. I remembered the little guy who'd said to a girlfriend of mine, 'Don't be so gentle, abuse me.' And she'd known a man in love with ropes who just wouldn't take yes for an answer. She'd told me of punters who, strangest of all, were just *into company*. Probably everyone had one secret, I decided, one skeleton. Robbie's friend, the Marigold, knew a woman who'd once asked a bloke to shit on her. I was almost smirking at it all, smirking at people more clandestine than me, more outside and more afraid. But, you know, I honestly couldn't have any doubt who my real enemy was. It was only myself. The ineluctable one. Didn't I take him here because I was just as twisted as anyone? I was the unique case of a female who, Robbie would later recount with a sneer, was into croaking deluded words like 'I care' and 'Aren't we good friends?' It was obvious.

I actually did buy something to improve the room. We actually did go into that junk shop with the skeleton beside the takeaway on Navarino Road. I had nicked off work one day by arrangement with Robbie, taken a coach to London, changed on it into an old anorak. On the way to the room he had the idea of going into the shop since it was open; I didn't particularly want to in case he broke something. There were some really psychotic things in there. He had a good howl and kept attracting the attention of the man at the counter. There was a wellington for sale. And pencil cases. He mucked about with them. And of course there were some of those dubious romantic prints of absolute tatterdemalions, so absurd. 'Look at that face,' I said, pointing one out. We laughed, it was so tearful. And oh, the sky was so fake. A white more glorious than anything you'd see in life. 'Male propaganda.' I shook my head. I'd noticed that concocted heaven plenty of times and it was no quintessence of any revelation, I can tell you. It was only a colour, a pale mud. I burst out laughing. God, sublimity was only a popular image. Robbie was getting attached to a plastic starfish framed behind glass. In the end we settled for it – it was a stupid-looking thing with one flat leg. The man wrapped it up in a paper bag. Working in a place like this, Robbie whispered, must make him really sick. He seemed okay to me, maybe a little bit gay, he looked like a woman who looked like a man. But then again, I thought, maybe he was really odd, his eyes were in the wrong place.

I wondered: what does he get up to in private? I carried our starfish in the paper bag as we walked to the room through a fragrance of varnish and late lingering wisteria daubed on a clumsy railing. He was happy for that moment. I wondered if I should take his hand just to look less like a dyke and more like a mother. But Hackney probably didn't disapprove of me at all. I suppose centuries had taught realism to the stoical, brooding façades. Occasional polluted oaks were like down-to-earth grandads. But there were also grudges in vigilant gardens where respectability clung on: umber silhouettes of tattered topiary of yew, and in some windows early Christmas trees trimmed to look false.

Then on our way up the stairs to the room we heard voices from the flat below us. A guy said, 'Leave off!'

'I don't know why we come here,' I groaned when I locked the door upstairs.

'Ah, he's all right.'

'What do you mean?' I said. I sat down beside him on the bed and looked at him long and hard like I was counting spots. 'Do you know him?' He got up and walked to the wardrobe. 'Do you?' I asked. He raised his eyebrows. I stood up. I hung the starfish on a nail already in the wall.

Nowadays I didn't know what to do, I'd just sit on the carpet flicking through a book I'd once bought him. Or sometimes I joked about the chastiser living below, holding young guys there, always touching. The afternoons were getting even darker. 'I know how to get your ring off,' I said once, trying to delay him on his way out, exactly like the chastiser.

'How?'

'Just cut the finger off.'

He was squeezing on his stinking trainers in a hurry. 'Wha'?'

'Don't worry,' I told him, 'it'll grow back.'
'Yeah, and your brain'll grow back one day.'
'Really?'
'Really, indeed, actually!'
'Nevertheless?'
He tied a lace. 'See you later, daddy.'
'See you,' I said.
'See you when I get me glasses.'

Another time I tried to entertain. I told him how once upon a time I used to dread going to the office, how I'd stay off sick. It was true. He was in a strange mood. He began to exhaust himself worrying me with a knuckle and giggling unhappily. I hadn't bothered to turn on the light. 'You want to walk before you can crawl,' I told him I was once reproached. I hadn't wanted to crawl. I would never wear a skirt and high-powered shoulders. They told me they felt I'd be happier if I left. He pinched my wrist. Oh, I wanted so much to hug him. But I wasn't the answer to his problems. I didn't see the point in loving him at all. In fact, I was thinking that we'd all be much better off without love anyway. I was coming round to seeing that my dad had been right about many things. He'd reached the conclusion that no one had the love they needed to be healthy, that everyone was just passing round their damage in the search for it. For years I'd quarrelled with him, called him life-denying and dogmatised and all the rest of it. But I wasn't so cocksure now. Everything was physical and left its mark. I quite liked this idea actually. That even virtues like love were pigments on the world's canvas like everything else, basically grubby. And I suppose my love was of a particularly grubby hue. As I sat thinking like this, and as Robbie lay perhaps thinking of whatever he loved and could never get, we looked up at that starfish.

I hated it. We called it Andy. 'How would they screw?'

Robbie asked. It was like a guy who never took his jacket off, I said. We could see him with this personality of his own: Andy who lived by himself in 75 Navarino Road, did his shopping in a twenty-four hour garage, sauntered slowly all the way there, would stand behind a young guy at the counter and pinch his arse, ate seafood at four o'clock at night, probably worked with polythene, took guys into his room and spanked them. The more I talked the more Robbie giggled. But I wasn't giggling. What would my dad have made of us sitting there? I suppose he would have worried in case we were spiritually doomed. Well, that didn't sound so bad.

One afternoon we'd hurried to the room without getting milk. I needed a coffee, I was going to nip out to the shop. He stood by the window obviously preferring the company of his shadow. A moth was battering the window. He had on a track-suit top that was too big for him, his cheek was pressed against the glass. 'We've no milk,' I said. I drew up behind him. Dandelions wagged under a vent.

'Someone's trying to open that window,' he told me.

'What?'

'Underneath us.'

I tried to peer down; I couldn't see anything. We searched each other's faces. I touched the collar of his top. I confessed to him how I believed the guy was holding someone in there. 'Raping him?' he said. It just felt like the sort of irritable day detectives would arrive and shout through a megaphone. Old dears would peer from the gate biting their lips. I stood beside him imagining. I saw us being implicated. 'What relation are you to this boy, madam?' I could see a brute in a raincoat with a bald, circumcised head. 'Aunt,' I'd assure him in my peachiest voice. The next thing Robbie would be locked up, I'd be held. I could see my home being done over, my secret discovered, polaroids of tortured girls slipped under my pillow. 'Confess!' A fat-mouthed dyke twisted my tit, a rusty lie detector rattled in. Terrible electrodes.

'Wha' time is it?' Robbie asked. I flattened his collar. He broke away. He sat on the bed. I sat down beside him. 'Don't go yet.' He stood up. He went to the window. I stood up. I asked did he want coffee. I fancied one. I suggested I could nip out for milk and on the way back steal a glance at the window, just to be on the safe side. He shrugged. Because of the mortice deadlock on my door you were forced to lock it when you left. 'I have to lock you in,' I explained as I threw my coat on, 'it doesn't close.' I asked him was that all right. He snapped at me: 'Wha'?' 'Look,' I said, 'I'll leave it open, I don't want you to think I'm locking you in.'

Luffing back from the shop through a shrill wind, I looked up at my gable. The curtains were open. I couldn't really see anything. Maybe it was silly. I didn't know what to think. Between two houses the sun was a very unconvincing brown circle. I clambered back up to the room. 'I don't know,' I laughed, 'there's nothing to see.' I tried to hide a simpering face. But Robbie wasn't there.

I hated myself for leaving the door open. Maybe the guy downstairs had taken him. I locked it. I listened to the flat below. It was quiet. I put the milk down. I took my coat off. He wasn't even wearing one. I scraped fluffy mould out of a cup and made coffee.

He didn't turn up next time. I didn't expect him to. But that didn't stop me worrying that something might be wrong or that he'd been locked up in that funny home. We'd talked about celebrating Christmas together but I didn't see him for the next few weeks so I didn't bother bringing down decorations for the room. Christmas passed. The last day I ever saw him was New Year's Eve. I decided to check the bus stop just in case. And he was leaning against it kitted out in a new jacket and jeans. I drew up. We were the only ones waiting. We stood staring at a lake that flooded half of the road. Navy clouds floated on it. The police skidded after a car in the distance. We turned to watch it. 'So long as they're not after us,' was the first thing I mumbled. At last a bus came wailing to a stop. By the time we got off it was dark. We didn't feel like talking and I didn't buy anything for him to eat. We went into the house. We listened as we passed the flat underneath us. At the top I opened the door of the room and he slumped on to the bed. I washed a cup as he smoked. 'Toast?' I whispered. He didn't answer. To start a conversation I said I wondered where the chastiser was, I didn't hear him below. I sat down on the edge of the bed with coffee. 'Maybe,' I said, 'he's been caught.' He didn't answer. I pretended to listen hard. He tweaked his eyelid. The nearest chimney was giving off wisps.

Then he said, 'Jackie.' I set my cup on the carpet. 'Would you not try it with a bloke?' I didn't answer. He didn't say anything more. My heart had got faster. I slipped on to the carpet. To distract from me a little I took the playing cards. I started building a factory. I hated those cards as a matter of fact. So did he. I completed two unsafe stages. Then I demolished them. He sat up on the bed. He spoke again. 'Just tell me, I don't mind.' I fumbled with the cards. 'Jackie?' I looked at him. 'Are you never into it?'

'What do you mean?' I stammered. His hand was resting near my arm.

'I'd do it.' He bit his nail.

'But,' I said. He was hanging his head, looking at the

bed. 'Look, I'm more like . . .' I listened for noises in the house. 'I'm sort of like . . . your old girl,' I whispered. He didn't say anything. 'Do you know what I mean?'

'Yeah.' He didn't move. Then he swung to his feet. He went to the door.

'Robbie,' I called from the bed. My head was pounding. I got up. I went and stood beside him. 'Listen.' There was a clamp on my throat. 'Be quiet as . . .' And I lifted my hand towards him. Now I just didn't care any more. He was watching me. Suddenly, I touched his head. I could hear my voice. '. . . as we're going out.' I was stroking his hair. 'Okay?' I was reeling. His tongue peeped out.

'Okay,' he whispered. I took my hand away. Then I opened the door. We went out. There was no one around.

We started walking to the bus. The night was calm. There was sand on the pavement. I waited for him at the stop on Navarino Road. 'So Sunday two weeks?' he said. I nodded. A crowd was leaving a house, the stereo was turned up. 'Can't I meet you next Sunday?' A bus was coming.

'Right,' I said quietly.

'When then?'

'When what?'

'Wha' day?'

'Well,' I smiled softly. 'Tuesdays and Fridays?'

He shook his head, grinning. He got on and I nodded to him at the window.

I walked back to the room. I'd nearly said to him, Be careful who you're with, Robbie. Be careful of weird people like me who want to get to know you. Inside I gathered the kettle and toaster, the two cups and plates and the cutlery, whatever coffee was left, the starfish from the wall, the playing cards, the book. I pulled the suitcase now wrapped with fine fluff out of the wardrobe. Everything fitted in it.

It was quiet in the house. I left the key on the oven and the room door lying open. I carried the suitcase all the way down to Mare Street to get the coach to Ipswich. There were taxis on the road. It was such a bright night. Perfect clouds were sitting.

THE SWEET SCENT OF ROMANCE

Tom Wakefield

Valerie Conway soon realised that it was better to lose a husband by way of death – natural or accidental – than by divorce. Her husband's heart attack and sudden demise had left her grief-stricken and desperately sad.

Now, four years after the event, she could look back on their time spent together as though it had been one long honeymoon. Her grief had dispersed amidst a social life which mostly centred around her work. Her part-time teaching (two and a half days a week at three different primary schools) was wholly satisfactory in terms of interest and economy.

'Never, I thought you were nearer forty at the most. How do you do it? You put Joan Collins to shame.'

'You're so broad-minded and interested in everyone.'

'The staff room is always livelier on Tuesdays, Valerie. You are like a breath of fresh air.'

'I do wish some of our younger colleagues were as punctual and prepared as you are, Mrs Conway . . .'

These unsought accolades imbued Valerie with a permanent sense of goodwill and satisfaction. She brimmed over with confidence. Popularity was her balm.

At fifty-three, perhaps more than ever, Valerie commanded attention; there was a marvellous spontaneity to her conversation. She presented a young, fresh sense of humour and the staff room bubbled with laughter when she was present.

'Darlings, that lovely Dean Rivers asked me to marry him today.'

'Did you give him any hope?'

'Well . . . well . . . I didn't say no. I said, "Finish reading this page." When he had struggled through it I said, "Dean, I am old enough to be your great-grandmother."'

'"I like my gran," he said. It's not every day one gets a proposal from a nine-year-old, is it?'

'If I got a marriage proposal from any man, I would begin to wonder what was wrong. Is he in debt? Does he have a string of broken marriages and battered wives in the background? Has he become a born-again Christian?'

On hearing this opinion, Valerie flicked one half of the yellow and brown silk scarf that adorned her throat so that one part hung comfortably over her left shoulder and one part hung over the front of her cream-coloured blouse.

Ann was such a dear, a kind, attractive – if a little overweight – young woman. It was a real sadness to meet such cynicism in a woman who was only just turned thirty. Valerie was about to chide her (in the gentlest possible way) when the bell rang to declare that lunch break was over. Instead she said, 'Would you like to come to dinner, Ann? Next Tuesday? I'm having a few friends around. Nothing elaborate.'

'I have my Turkish class that night.'

'What time does it finish?'

'Oh, six-ish.'

'Come straight after your class then. Turkish first, delight afterwards.'

Valerie's laughter at her own remark gave Ann no further chance to defer attendance.

'P.P.G.A.A.,' Valerie murmured into the reflection which faced her in the bathroom mirror. 'Preparation, presentation, generalisation and application.' She had remembered the letters and the words they represented from her early teacher-training on classroom technique. They provided a

[170]

framework for the successful lesson. Valerie used the same formula for her dinner parties at her house in Bounds Green.

In giving pleasure to others through the comforts of her North London house she managed to achieve a great deal of personal satisfaction. Why, in just over two and a half years, no fewer than three couples had begun their first tentative steps which eventually led them to the register office and marriage.

She transferred her art of gentle, beguiling skill at organised control from her classroom to her home; just as her pupils learned to read without realising it, so some of her guests had been ensnared in romantic affiliation. For Valerie, admission or acceptance of the single state boded a future of desolation for any man or woman who chose to settle for it.

A trace of light blue eye-shadow, carefully applied from the small pot to her little finger then on to each eyelid, completed her cosmetic preparations.

Her loose-fitting navy blue dress was modest, as was her pale pink lipstick. She chose to wear no jewellery save for a thin gold chain about her throat and a bracelet of similar austerity about her wrist.

With her blonde hair swept away from her face and coiled at the back in one of those chignon hair-do's much favoured by royal princesses attending tennis events, she descended the stairs with her tuberose perfume floating all about her, in a state of ineffable femininity.

The guests were not due for at least an hour but the house was ready for them – prepared, like its owner; it exuded a serenity and calm which would please and envelop. The dining places were set around the glass-topped circular table which stood near the french windows that opened on to the patio and lawn.

It was one of those rare June evenings which are more reminiscent of the Mediterranean than Britain. They would dine by candlelight – perhaps they might open the windows fully and look out at the garden.

There would be four courses. They would start with cold sorrel soup, then go on to the salmon mayonnaise, salad and new potatoes. A pause, a long pause, then some sliced honeydew melon, followed by Brie and biscuits.

But first she would show her guests into the lounge, its subdued lighting and comfortable chairs (strategically placed around the gold-coloured coffee table) affording a social proximity conducive to harmony. Not that Valerie believed falling in love happened suddenly. The bolt of lightning passion, or Cupid's dart, delivered only disaster as far as she was concerned. No. Love had to be laboured for – and some people had no aptitude for such skilled work.

Outwardly, Valerie bore her widowhood with a brave, sad acceptance. She would talk of her husband in gentle, hushed tones – of the perfection of their pairing.

'Barry and I never quarrelled, you see. We each knew what the other was thinking – I'm not overtly religious – but there was a kind of mystic communion between us. The moment we saw this house we knew it was right for us – we didn't have to discuss it. He smiled and I nodded, and that was it.'

She believed this account, rendered in affectionate recall. In fact, she had said, 'I could never settle in this area.'

He had shrugged his shoulders and smirked with exasperation. 'It's this or a larger flat – it's all the same to me. The part of London you want to live in is beyond our pocket. Please yourself.'

'Mmm . . . mmm . . . Well, I suppose we could make something of it . . . and it's very central . . . perhaps we could sell at a profit later and set our sights on something more . . . it does have a lovely garden. . . .'

Not only had she remained in Bounds Green, she had come to adore it. The admixture of prosperous Greeks and middle-pay-range professional workers gave the terraced houses a certain neatness and order that other parts of London seemed to lack. Window panes sparkled, gardens (both front and back) were carefully tended. There were no beggars and the children did not use bad language in the street.

The children . . . Tonight Valerie would view Ann with all the maternal tenderness that still resided in her sweet-smelling bosom.

She had always expected pregnancy – had relished the idea of announcing it to Barry – had looked forward to lactating breasts. On her thirty-fifth birthday she had visited a gynaecologist and was assured (after a battery of tests) that she was as fertile as any other woman of her age. She had broached the subject with Barry.

'Look, darling,' he had said consolingly, 'it isn't going to happen. Aren't I enough?'

She had cried a little. 'I want to hold a baby. My baby . . . our baby.'

'I'm your baby.' He had placed his arm about her as he spoke. 'Hold me.'

'We can afford it,' she persisted.

'It's not a question of what we can afford. It won't happen.'

'I've been for tests. I *can* have a baby. Perhaps if you went along too we could try – '

'Stop!' He had been abrupt, harsh even. 'I don't want a baby – I hate the smell of them. I loathe their noise – their incessant demands – their dribbling mouths and farting little bums,' he shouted. 'I don't want to hold one either.'

'But if it happened . . . it might . . . it might still . . . you would have to – '

'It won't happen. I got myself snipped. It was when you were selling your mother's house in Solihull.'

'You asked me to stay on longer . . . hold out for a higher price . . . you bought time for a vasectomy.' She had not been able to veil the accusing tone behind her words.

He had left the room without saying any more. Neither of them liked 'scenes' even if 'scenes' were required.

She had sat and wept. She had always wondered how she would cope with adultery if ever it arose – it never had; a passing betrayal (she was sure) she could forgive. But this, this was so complete a thing. Perhaps it was at this point in time when the house itself became more important than the man she lived in it with.

Now that he was gone, she enjoyed, more than ever, drifting from room to room. The furniture, the pictures, the curtains, the carpets, the correct kind of beaded lampshade, emerged before her gaze as though she were gliding through the wonders of a coral reef.

Like any good director, Valerie knew how to set her stage; as the doorbell chimed she pressed the start button on the tape-recorder and, to a background of popular operatic arias, she opened the door.

'What lovely music you have, Valerie. It makes a change from Nana Mouskouri. I wish my mother would have a love affair with Callas.'

'Come in, Lakis. You shouldn't have brought this.' Valerie took the bottle from him as she led him into the hallway. 'Do go in the lounge, you are the first to arrive.' She held the bottle close to the lampshade so that the light caused its pale yellow colour to glow. 'Aphrodite – a lovely name for a wine.'

'It's very dry,' said Lakis.

Valerie always experienced a slight sense of aesthetic shock when Lakis opened his mouth and spoke. With his lean, equine, pale face and sad, dark eyes he looked as if he had been extracted from some early Greek icon and placed in modern dress. His black hair and grave expression put her in mind of Mount Athos, whereas his London accent, fawn-coloured cotton trousers and stated affection for the Arsenal football team placed him closer to his birthplace which had been Kentish Town.

'I'd love to go back and live where I was born,' he had once casually remarked to Valerie over the garden fence which overlooked her lawn.

'Oh, I love Greece. Barry and I hopped islands together many years ago. Mykonos, Aegina, Tinos, Poros . . . the memory of those places still haunts me. I've heard that they are quite ruined now. Too many tourists have destroyed the charm of the – '

Valerie was cut short as Lakis dispelled her romantic train of thought and babble.

'Kentish Town, Mrs Conway. I'd like to live in Kentish Town. I don't want to live on an island – Kentish Town is where I was born. I think it would make you happy if we kept goats in the back garden.'

She ushered him into the lounge and waved a hand in the direction of the chair in which she wanted him to sit.

'You'll excuse me, Lakis – just a few things to set right in the dining-room. The others should be here at any moment now – I like to have as much prepared beforehand as possible.'

Apart from lighting the candles there was really nothing more to do in the dining-room. Everything was ready except things had gone a little awry. She had asked Ann to arrive at 7 p.m., Lakis at 7.15, and Richard at 7.30 – the order of arrival had now been disrupted. She had so wanted Ann in the lounge first . . . greetings were so important.

She was given very little further time for minor regret as the door chimes heralded the arrival of her second guest barely after Lakis had sat down. Richard apologised for not wearing a jacket or tie – the warmth of the evening had overcome his mild sense of formality. Before he entered, Ann's voice, from the other side of the road, indicated to Valerie that all her guests had arrived.

Valerie delivered introductions as though she were pre-senting a mini curriculum vitae on each person. She divulged that she had known Lakis since he was twelve years of age, that his mother was her next-door neighbour, that he ran a small travel company which specialised in tours of the Middle East, and – half-laughingly – that he had broken the hearts of at least three Greek girls whom his mother had thought suitable for marriage.

She sketched in Richard's north of England background, mentioned that he was twenty-eight years of age and had already been short-listed for three deputy headships. She managed to hint that a certain sloppiness in his mode of dress seemed to imply that he needed 'looking after'.

Alighting on Ann as though she were a nasturtium bloom awaiting some friendly bee, Valerie portrayed a lovely, sweet-natured, hard-working woman with hidden recesses of honey ready to be sipped.

The ice in their glasses of vodka and tonic clinked out a happy overture as Valerie beamed out these appraisals.

'And now, if you'll give me fifteen minutes or so, I'll get back to the dining-room. Lakis, you know the way through, I'll call out when I'm ready.' She was careful to leave the lounge door ajar as she left. 'It may be a little warm in here,

I'll leave the french windows open in the dining-room – you'll feel the breeze in here.'

On entering the kitchen-cum-dining-room, Valerie lowered the volume on the tape of 'One Fine Day' (the melody and the lyrics had such an air of expectancy about them), she lit the candles and sighed with pleasure. The flames changed the glasses and bottles of wine into instant *objets d'art*. Lastly, she opened the french windows and inhaled the sweet and heady nocturnal scents of the great clumps of nicotiana and flowering honeysuckle.

At this point Valerie settled herself calmly in the bay window seat and listened to the conversation from the lounge. Of course, she thought, they would be struggling to find some common ground for discussion. It was always the way when unaffiliated men met unaffiliated women. Valerie enjoyed eavesdropping on such awkward reconnoitring.

She felt hopeful; Ann appeared to have made an 'effort'. The floral blouse and culottes to match were colourful without being vulgar, and her hair, which often resembled a frizzy frame about her face, had been swept up high and piled on top of her head to a better, and indeed slimmer, effect.

On the other hand, Richard's sparse beard, faded khaki, baggy trousers and shabby unironed shirt convinced Valerie that he bought all his clothes from a charity shop. It was as if he contrarily sought to conceal his height and blond good looks by a dowdy choice of apparel.

She glanced at her watch – give them fifteen minutes. Wait until she had counted at least three gaps of uncomfortable silence in the chit-chat.

After ten minutes Valerie felt the need to change her tactics; there had been no silences. Conversation had continued effortlessly, amiably. And now she could hear laughter and merriment which was more in line with what was expected of a family Christmas gathering rather than three people who barely knew one another.

Struggling to keep out the trace of pique which wanted to creep into her tone she called out, 'Dinner is ready.'

'How lovely,' Ann murmured appreciatively when they were all seated.

From this point on Valerie decided she would direct the conversation. Three amusing school anecdotes, an account of her last holiday on Crete, and the merits of the TV serialisation of *Middlemarch* would take them well into the main course. Valerie preferred to entertain rather than be entertained – this was, after all, her home. She was, like any good teacher, entitled to control events and discussion.

'. . . so I said, but Joey . . . "Cockles and mussels" isn't a rude song. Cockles and mussels are shellfish, we find them at the seaside. Well, he shook his little head and turned his big, dark brown eyes upon me. "No, Mrs Conway – my mum heard one of my older brothers using one of those words, one of the words you just said, and she slapped his face – she was angry with him . . ."'

Valerie was somewhat disappointed with the subdued responses from her guests. It almost seemed as if Ann wilfully sought to change the subject by her observation.

'Oh look, there are fires being lit out there. Out there in the gardens close by. Maybe three or four.'

'Barbecues,' Lakis groaned.

As bouzouki music floated in through the open doors Valerie began her verbal tour of her holiday in Crete. Once again (as her guests enjoyed the salmon mayonnaise) her flow was interrupted by the unexpected.

Richard drew their attention to the three or four exceedingly large moths which had been enticed indoors by the dancing candle flames.

'Perhaps we'd better close the doors?'

Valerie ignored his question by quietly offering him a little more salmon.

She began to extol the virtues of the mountain towns and villages of Crete as opposed to over-developed coastal tourist towns. Her three guests were quietly dutiful but their attention was entirely taken up by the impending hara-kiri of the largest of the moths.

It hovered – it advanced – it retreated – it advanced once more, getting closer and closer to the candle flame. Valerie seemed unaware of its existence but suddenly caught her breath in conversational flow as the creature fizzed, popped and finally combusted. Tiny bits of debris fell about the table.

Due to the loud wailing sound of the bouzouki music flowing from neighbouring gardens table talk was now being conducted on a louder decibel than was normal for such occasions. The strong smell of barbecued chops, spiced sausages, and grilled chicken from outside now pervaded the dining area.

By the time the Brie was being served, a gentle evening breeze had begun to waft in great clouds of smoke. Valerie did not admit defeat and close the door until Ann broke into a fit of coughing and Richard's eyes began to redden and break into tears.

'I wonder if you three would like to take your coffee in the lounge? I can bring it in to you, it's no extra bother, I won't be long.'

Her guests thought this an excellent idea and staggered from the table, none of them feeling the slightest bit selfish.

Valerie closed the french windows and shut out the noises

of the night. As her percolator gently bubbled she heard animated talk and shrieks of laughter coming from the lounge. The merriment seemed to have a ribald flavour to it. In her wildest hopes she had not expected Ann to get on *this* well with the two men. A woman of a less generous nature might have felt somewhat jealous. Yet it did seem to her that her guests seemed happier when their hostess was not present.

As she poured the coffee into the four awaiting cups she suddenly felt quite horribly redundant. When she entered the lounge it felt as if she were a guest. Lakis took the tray from her. Richard offered her his chair, and Ann insisted on passing the cups around.

By half-past ten the evening was at an end; all the guests had tactfully agreed that work pressures of the morrow required an early night. Valerie was pleasantly surprised by the sincere and warm thanks that her guests extended to her. Perhaps the evening had been more successful than she had imagined after all. Any doubts she had harboured were truly dispelled when the three guests exchanged telephone numbers.

The washing-up chores seemed to pass quickly. In spite of the atmosphere in the kitchen (still reeking of burnt flesh) Valerie sniffed the sweet smell of romance. By the time the last plate was stacked away Valerie had begun to wonder what she might wear for the future wedding. Would they ask her to be matron of honour? In which case a new outfit would be called for.

That night she slept soundly; in her dreams she saw herself in an oyster-grey silk suit. And pearls, pearls everywhere – about her throat, entwined in her hair – she smiled into their dull, welcoming glow.

For the next three weeks Valerie waited patiently for the messenger who would relay the onset of the romance.

Would Richard mention it at school? Might Lakis' mother (her face full of joy) whisper the good news through the lattice fence? Would Ann (her complexion slightly flushed) mention it to her in the corridor that led to their classrooms? And which of the men would she settle for?

After almost a month Valerie began to feel less confident. She began to feel cheated, so much effort . . . and nothing. Nothing.

The postcard, when it arrived said little but expressed a great deal.

Dear Valerie,

Thank you for bringing us together, it has made such a difference to our lives and we are both blissfully happy. Would you be free to come to dinner with us on Wednesday 18th – 7 p.m? We do hope you can make it.

Best wishes, Richard.

Valerie answered discreetly in the form of a notelet with matching decorated envelope. 'She was delighted to accept the invitation.'

On the Monday before the dinner she sought to engage Ann in polite conversation hoping for some frisson of information pertaining to Richard. Instead, Ann had merely talked on about the virtues of a mixed reading scheme as opposed to choosing either phonic or 'look and say'. Then, almost as an afterthought, Ann had smiled and said, 'Oh, I'll see you tomorrow, tomorrow night at Richard's.

Valerie had nodded knowingly and all but whispered, 'I'm looking forward to it, my dear.'

From the way Ann had casually thrown her cardigan over the back of the settee, Valerie knew that this was not her first visit to Richard's flat. There was a domestic familiarity between the two of them which hinted to Valerie that their knowledge of one another had already gone beyond holding hands or kissing. Had Ann stayed overnight here? Or had she moved?

Valerie's exciting speculation was interrupted by Lakis who burst into the room full of apology.

'I'm sorry I'm late, another bomb scare on the Tube, we were held up for nearly an hour at King's Cross. I felt the need of a shower.'

His appearance in a white towelling bathrobe, the hair on his head and legs still glistening in their wetness, caused her to feel as if someone had planted a hand grenade behind the cushion of her chair. She leant forward as Lakis called out to the kitchen.

'I'll dress now, Richard. Just give me two minutes and I'll be down to give you a hand.' He kissed Ann on the forehead and then turned to Valerie. 'Richard is doing the main course, I'm preparing the starters – you like calamaris?'

'Yes, oh yes,' Valerie muttered and then with one gulp, swallowed all the sherry that remained in her glass.

Valerie had always expressed a liberality of outlook as far as sexual preferences were concerned but throughout the meal that followed her feelings failed to match her stated opinions. She felt as if her own powers of perception had been assaulted, she felt betrayed by some grand type of duplicity. Nevertheless she managed to camouflage what she felt and presented an external front of contented composure. Thankfully, the other three talked so much, she was required to do little more than smile and eat.

When her minicab arrived to take her she spoke to Richard who had gallantly opened the cab door for her. She sought to offer him a mild rebuke, a small punishment for his unorthodox state of happiness. Place a social sanction on it.

'It's a pity about poor Ann. She must be lonely. Such a lovely girl.'

'Alone? Ann alone?' Richard had looked puzzled and then had said, 'But she is settled, she and Elaine have been together for eight years.'

Valerie sank into the back of the car, smiled bravely and waved as the vehicle drew slowly away from the kerb.

As the car sped towards Bounds Green she peered out from the windows in search of familiar landmarks along the route home. Such was the extent of her present state of disorientation, she had begun to feel a little lost.

LA TRICOTEUSE

Monica Furlong

Nowadays I quite often dream of the City. In my sleep I walk through the ancient alleyways and across the cobbled streets, I watch the fast-flowing river from the bridge. I see the spire and patterned roof of St Saviour's rising behind the steep rooftops, my eye follows the turrets and buttresses. I look again at the shifting lights of the huge rose window.

Memory is the only place where that city still exists. War destroyed it, though by then Raoul and I were long gone.

We spent two years in the City together, a newly married husband and wife, passionately in love. Raoul was twenty-five and I was twenty-two. Offered a job teaching French at the university in the City he had said to me, 'Would you be happy so far from home?' and I had said, 'Of course. It would be an adventure.'

'But what will you do while I teach?'

It was simple. The City, which owned one of the most famous art galleries in the world – a former king had had a passion for the Flemish and German masters – offered an apprenticeship in picture restoration. We could just afford the fee.

'We shall be poor,' said Raoul.

'We shan't need much.'

So Raoul spent his days at the university, and I spent them studying pictures, or learning how to remove coats of varnish yellowed and cracked by the passing years. On my first day I learned the value of human spit – enzyme is a great natural dissolvant. Other bodily excretions were useful too.

The university lent us an apartment, not, unfortunately, in a medieval house, but in a pleasant modern block. It was built around a quadrangle with a small square garden that came to life when the harsh winter eventually left us. Looking from our window we could see a series of windows on a level with our own.

I am tempted to say that Raoul and I were idyllically happy in our new life but that would not be quite true. We were more homesick for family and friends, and even for familiar food, than either of us admitted. It was tiring trying to speak a new language all the time, never being articulate except with each other. But the absolute foreignness with which we were surrounded gave a sharpness and flavour to our perceptions, as if our senses were attuned by the unfamiliarity of daily life. The strange smells and sights and the new words used successfully by us often gave us a sort of ecstasy. But sometimes we would catch ourselves longing for a dull day in England, or, in Raoul's case, for a sunny day in the Midi. In the main, though, I think the sense of our alienation, of the looming loneliness, intensified our pleasure in being together, safe in the fortress of love.

We explored untiringly. On Sundays we often went to Mass in the Gothic glory of St Saviour's, and then we would walk for miles along the willowy banks of the great river, coming back on a tiny toy train with smoke wreathing through the tunnels. Before the snows came we tramped in the mountains, offered meals by lonely farmers' wives who would cook us food for a small payment and for the pleasure of our inept conversation. When we got home after hours of exercise in the open air we were still not too tired to make love – we were never too tired in those days. Our physical loving was an open secret, a lunatic delight, a joke, a spring of invention and imagination that seemed inexhaustible. In my mind I can still see Raoul's face transformed by love-

making, the flickering of passion in his eyes. And he used
to tease me afterwards: 'You can't go out with that look on
your face. It's indecent. Everyone would know at once!'
But we went out just the same, eating, drinking, walking.
Once we found ourselves in a smoky underground tavern
full of sailors and women. As we peered through the smoke
we thought that the women were prostitutes – there were
many prostitutes in the City. But as we waited for a drink,
and didn't get served, it gradually dawned on us that the
women were men. It surprised our innocence. In a con-
certed movement, without judgement or curiosity, we got
up and left, and oddly enough never even talked about it.
Things felt foreign enough just then.

The core of our life was in the apartment with its simple
chores, as we cooked and ate and tidied up and chatted and
made love together. In an apartment across the quadrangle
we often noticed another couple sharing a married life. She
was in her forties, he, we thought, in his fifties, and there
were no children. At first we did not notice them much
except when they were eating dinner. Their table was
always carefully laid in the window of their sitting-room –
it was possible from our look-out to see the white glow of
the cloth and the glimmer of glass and silver. There was a
rather ugly lamp which stood on the table as the evenings
grew darker. The couple ate formally – at least three
courses, with wine, followed by cheese and liqueurs, and
they were waited on by a servant. Inevitably, they were
stout, given up to the heaviness of middle years. Raoul
insisted that they rarely spoke to each other. 'They have
been married for so long there is no longer anything to say!'
Certainly, so far as we could see, they ate without exchang-
ing a word. There was no animation, no life. After dinner,
when the servant had cleared the table, the woman would
continue to sit by the window, knitting, knitting. We could

not see what she knitted – a mass of white or pink froth it appeared from where we sat. 'Bedjackets!' I said scornfully.

Sometimes the man would stand at the table beside her, his hands behind his back, staring vacantly out into darkness; by this time the quadrangle had filled with darkness, and their window floated, like a small boat of light on the twilight sea. There was something a little frightening about him, as of huge power frustrated or held in reserve, and also a sense of melancholy. Safe in our happiness we pitied the silent couple.

And mocked them. Raoul bestowed nicknames on them. Of course, they had to have names – they were so much a part of our lives – but the names were grim ones, perhaps reflecting the sense of threat their apparent apathy together gave to our youthful lives. Or perhaps not. Maybe it was simply unimaginable to us that we should grow old and our love might cool. Anyway, Raoul called the woman 'La Tricoteuse', and the man 'Bonaparte on Elba', though we later shortened this to the old British title for the arch-enemy – 'Boney'. Night after night, as we ate our modest suppers, we observed Boney and La Tricoteuse and speculated about them.

'What do you think he does for a living?'

'Retired, I suppose. He is around at all hours of the day.'

'But sometimes not at all. Sometimes she knits alone.'

'He is out with his cronies, perhaps?'

It seemed unlikely. He did not seem like 'a man's man'. She, we had no doubt, was a dull *hausfrau*.

'Her linen cupboard is immaculate,' Raoul said.

'She could tell you how many spoons she has.'

'And what the servant spends on food, down to the last centime.'

We laughed. We were terrible housekeepers. Raoul knew that I should never achieve the *bienséance* of a French housewife, and was glad that we were far away from his mother and sisters so that I could not be judged by them.

'Do you think he beats her?' Raoul asked. 'I think he never allows her to go out.' Neither of us had ever seen her in the street.

'He is tyrannical!'

'But she loves it! It makes her polish her spoons all the harder, just for him.'

'Perhaps the sex is better after he has beaten her.'

'Oh really? Is that a suggestion?'

And we were back to our bed and our tireless love-making.

The winter wore on. Raoul taught his students, I was entrusted with my first real painting to clean, a Flemish painting which no apprentice of my inexperience would be allowed to touch nowadays. It had its effect. I had a chance to study it day after day – the Virgin's spare pair of shoes tucked under a chair in the corner, the Infant's little vest hanging before the fire to air. Being entrusted with some-thing so important – like a child allowed to handle a precious family heirloom – I brought to it a huge awe, a devotional love. I worked with infinite care (under strict supervision), sometimes not quite sure where the painting ended and I began. I felt as if I was inside it.

So that when in spring I said that I thought I should see a doctor, Raoul joked that it was the painting that had made me pregnant. He enquired among his university colleagues and came up with a respected name.

'Your supposition is correct, madame,' the doctor said within a few minutes. 'I congratulate you.' He gave me some advice about general care of myself, and then asked where I proposed to have the confinement.

'At the apartment,' I said. He conducted himself politely, as expensive doctors do, and said he thought he should give me some idea of the cost of regular visits to him and a home confinement.

'I couldn't afford that,' I said finally, and he was too well bred to say 'I thought not.'

'There are two alternatives,' he said. 'There are other doctors, of course. And there is the public hospital. The other doctors . . .?'

I had seen the public hospital, a wicked-looking charitable foundation that I suspected (rightly) stank of antiseptic and ether. The doctor saw my expression and went on, 'Do not despise St Victor's, madame. There is a famous obstetrician, one of the greatest in the world, who gives his services there, two, three days a week. You could not have better care if you were the Queen of England. I would send my own daughter to him.'

Knowing the pressures of professional rivalry, I thought it must indeed be a fatherly feeling that inspired him.

'His name is Stefan Lacinski. Be sure and ask to see him.'

I lay resentfully in a cubicle at St Victor's. The yellowing and cracked walls filled me with distaste, but I noticed that the sheet on the bed was clean and the floor had been polished. It was a long wait, however, I was tired from walking about the city, and despite my apprehension, I dozed off. I woke abruptly when someone came into the cubicle, and opening my eyes was amazed to see it was Boney.

'I am Stefan Lacinski,' he began, and then his voice faltered. 'I know you from the apartments.' He laughed, a warm, pleasant laugh. 'Forgive me. We, my wife and I, we call you the Young Lovers.'

I was silent with surprise, mostly at seeing him at all, but also at what he was saying. It had never occurred to me that Boney and La Tricoteuse, apparently so indifferent, observed us as we observed them, though they had found something kinder to say about us. In his white coat, and in conversation, Boney seemed much livelier and slimmer than in his melancholy times of brooding at the window of his flat.

'It must seem grim to you here, even alarming,' he went on, 'but I have managed to obtain much stricter standards of hygiene. Even the equipment is not bad now. I brought some with me from Russia and I was able to buy some cheaply . . .' He had been there two years, he said, and he was gradually changing it.

'I have this boyish vision, this ridiculous idealism,' he said with a deprecating face, 'that by changing obstetrics we might change the world. But only women believe me.'

I went home to Raoul with a story to tell and he listened with rapt attention. We were somewhat embarrassed when, once again, we saw Boney and La Tricoteuse dining at their window, but this time, when we had sat down to our own meal, Boney turned and raised his glass to us with a smile.

We soon learned that Boney had not told us the whole truth. Raoul's colleagues had heard of the famous Stefan Lacinski – everybody seemed to know about him but us. He had left his own country and gone to work in Russia in the early years after the Revolution fired by a passionate belief in a classless state. In those days he was less interested in obstetrics than in genetic planning – he saw himself as a researcher rather than a practising doctor. Because of his international eminence he was a feather in the cap of the system. He had been given fine research facilities, an apartment in Moscow, a dacha in the country. Then, Raoul's informants did not quite know why, he had fallen foul of the authorities, or perhaps simply ceased to believe in the system. He had become more and more interested in obstetrics, less and less interested in laboratory work, and finally had left Russia and come to work in the City. He saw a few private patients, but his main work was at St Victor's. There he assisted at the *accouchements* of farm girls and slum women, and he had started a programme, financed by some of his wealthy patients, to provide better food for poor mothers who were pregnant.

'Fancy our Boney being so special!' said Raoul when he told me all this.

I went at regular intervals to the public hospital and was usually examined by Lacinski himself. When the confinement drew near he said, 'My wife wondered if you would care to dine with us one evening. She is an invalid, you know, and she does not see many people. I hope this is not an abuse of the professional relationship, but you must feel free to refuse if it feels awkward.'

On the contrary, I assured him. It would not feel awkward at all. Raoul and I would be delighted.

'Tanya will be so pleased. You'll see inside the magic window at last,' he added with a touch of mischief. 'I'm afraid we're really awfully dull.' I blushed a little when he said this, but I hoped he didn't notice.

Tanya, we soon saw, was quite severely crippled – that had not been apparent as we watched her through the window. The grim expression that had given her her nickname disappeared as soon as she talked. Once, it was clear, she had been a pretty woman – she still had fine blue eyes, although her hair was white. She spoke wonderful English – the first I had spoken since I left home – Raoul and I talked French together; her French was excellent too. She came, we soon realised, from the sort of well-to-do pre-Revolution Russian family who spoke French at home as a matter of course and had an English or Scottish nanny for the children.

'Come again!' she said as we left, and we did, running in for drinks before supper or for tea on Sundays. Once we invited them back for a meal but their exchange of glances and his quick refusal showed that it was apparent the venture was beyond her. It was not so much, we guessed, that the walk around the balcony was too much, but that she had become confined in all senses to her home – to go beyond her apartment felt unthinkable, desperately unsafe. We conveniently forgot that we had called the two of them La Tricoteuse and Boney. We felt fond of them, we noted their quiet enjoyment of each other, we found them light, funny, intelligent in conversation. To a young couple a long way from family and home, they became the elderly ballast that we lacked in our lives – parents, aunts, uncles.

Yet there was much we did not know about them.

'Do you have children?' I asked Tanya once.

'No, no children,' she said, and I thought perhaps they had been too old when they came together to think of it.

Stefan was with me during my confinement, and I had a daughter, with Raoul's beautiful southern looks. She lived for only two days. Her heart was no good, there was no way to keep her alive. All that long gestation, all that struggle to give birth, all that hope and joy, and it was useless, pointless.

The convalescence was slow and dreadful. I had no heart to get better. It was as if the loss of the baby had poisoned the love between me and Raoul, or had shown it to be no good. Even when I was over the birth we no longer made love; we scarcely spoke to one another. God had cheated me, I felt.

Stefan was gentle.

'It will be slow. One day you will have another child . . . Why not go back to the gallery? It would be something else to think of.' But I clung on to my grief as if it was all that I had.

Weeks later, as I was sitting at home staring vacantly into

space, I heard a tapping sound. I could not at first think
where it came from, and then I looked at the french window
that gave on to the balcony of the flats. To my astonishment
I saw Tanya Lacinska standing outside the window, supporting herself uncertainly with one hand against the
window, the other holding a stick.

'Tanya, you came to see me!' I said, more touched than
I knew how to say, as I helped her to a chair.

'For heartbreak anything is possible,' she said simply.

I do not remember everything we said to one another,
only how whatever was said was transformed by the huge
effort she had made to come at all. She carried a small
parcel.

'I did not know whether to give this to you, but it seemed
to me it might be a promise for the future.'

I undid the parcel and found inside it a baby's shawl
beautifully knitted, a gossamer web. My grandmother was
a Shetland woman and I knew of their famous shawls –
'They can pass through a wedding ring,' she used to say to
me proudly. This shawl was the first I had ever seen that
was as fine. I wept, more with love than grief perhaps, and
then I heard myself making a sort of confession, about the
way Raoul and I used to call her La Tricoteuse. She became
completely silent for a while.

'It is odd you should say that. When I was in the camp
we women used to make ourselves clothes out of scraps of
material – cloths for cleaning, bits and pieces people left
behind. I was the knitting expert, I made wonderful things
out of worn-out jumpers – it was an irony that I had once
been a designer in Paris, but that took less ingenuity than
trying to dress us all out of scraps. There was a Latvian
woman in our group who used to call me that – La
Tricoteuse. We had more jokes than you might imagine.

'It was because of the camp,' she went on, 'that I had no

children. You know, they had a punishment device they called "the Freezer". They put you in this small hole in which the temperature of the body was reduced to a dangerous level. For women – they warned us of this – it might mean that you lost your fertility. I was,' she went on 'a kind of leader of our group, and I made up my mind that every time they, the guards, transgressed decent human behaviour with one of us, I would make a quiet, rational protest. It was an expensive decision.' She paused for a long time. 'They would have killed me, I think, but Stefan got me out. On the pretence that he needed women who had had this experience for his experiments in fertility he took me, and a number of other women away. He had heard of the device and was determined to defy it. For Stefan, you know, babies are sacred.' She was silent for a long while, thinking, I suppose, of Stefan, and then she went on, 'Much later we were married.'

'What's that?' Raoul asked when he came home, seeing the exquisite shawl lying over the back of a chair.

'A present from La Tricoteuse,' I told him.

I went back to the gallery the next day, to the picture of the baby's little vest airing before the fire and the Virgin's shoes tucked under the chair. It was only when I had worked on the Virgin's face for some time that I realised that she reminded me of Tanya, which seemed odd. I suppose it was because she had given me new life.

FOR TWO
PIANOS

Daniel Moyano

translated by Norman Thomas di Giovanni
and Susan Ashe

It was back in the halcyon days, the heroic age of Herminio Torres Brizuela, the then governor of La Rioja, who on Sundays toured the province inaugurating electric light factories, embracing every second person, and at the same time consuming a great deal of barbecued kid; and who, through the good offices of Cholo Lanzillotto, the sweetest of ministers, enabled us to form a quartet, so that while Herminio electrified the Argentine countryside we serenaded it.

Irma had just produced our son Ricardo, at the very moment when Carlos Cáceres, the Parisian-La Rioja painter, who was director of culture for the province, gave us the go-ahead to set up a *conservatoire* and a quartet. So it was that our son came into the world, as it were, with a *conservatoire* under one arm.

We were living in an old house in Rivadavia Street (named after Argentina's first president, who ended his days in Cádiz, in Spain, where his now semi-derelict house can still be seen) which was so hot that you had to leave the front door open at night to let a breath of air in. One time a couple of the donkeys that roamed the streets sniffing round dustbins for paper came in and ate seven of my best stories. I was never able to reconstruct them, but they must be out there somewhere, running around in animal memory, to what end goodness only knows.

Irma had a piano at her parents' house in Morteros, far to the south on the edge of the humid pampa, a Krämer that had come by ship from Europe, packed in lead sheets that must have cost almost as much as the instrument itself and crated in a box of fir planks that struck us as an extravagance. You can't imagine how the piano trembled with emotion, remembering its *Vaterland*, whenever anyone played 'O Tannenbaum' on it.

Even its packing case was musical, what with its *Tannenbaum* wood, from the European Christmas tree, and snow and carols and 'Stille Nacht, heilige Nacht'. However you looked at it, the Krämer was music. Irma's family had promised to send it on to us should some relative with a lorry happen to be travelling in our out-of-the-way direction, but the years came and went, and the piano never arrived. We left room for it − out of reach of intruding donkeys, of course. So sure were we that it would one day turn up − and so used to its virtual presence − that, to avoid bumping into it, we never trod in the place it somehow occupied. One day we turned down I forget what piece of furniture that someone wanted to give us, since the only room we had for it was where the piano was to go. The gift's lowly status (I think it was a wardrobe) and garish colour would have dimmed the lustre of the Krämer.

Krämer. A word that reminded me of a line from Rilke that spoke of '*Musik der Kräfte*', or music of power. The piano's name and remoteness gave it tremendous power. At home, my one little violin playing unaccompanied, was pure sadness. But the day the Krämer arrived, my music (I was learning Corelli's 'La Follia' for the quartet competition) − well, the instrument might turn me into the Topolski of La Rioja. The one thing against me was my name. Moyano is altogether wrong for a violinist. At best, it's a name for the owner of a wine shop ('Kids, run and fetch the wine from don Moyano's') and at worst, a knife-fighter from the Firpo or Güemes neighbourhoods of

Córdoba ('Watch it, pal, here comes the Indian Moyano, and when he's got a knife on him he can be fairly lethal').

In my musician days, however, I went about the tough neighbourhoods of Córdoba playing the mandolin, and the only weapon I carried was my instrument. One dark night in the part of town called Talleres Este, which was full of brawling drunks, I had to break off in order to dodge flying bottles. When the fracas was over and the owner of the place asked me to go on playing so as to help restore calm, I said, 'Hand me my weapon,' which had been knocked out of my hands and was rolling around underfoot. When they heard the word 'weapon', two of the local lads drew their knives again, believing I was about to attack them. All I was about to attack was a Peruvian waltz that was the rage at the time.

One day when Irma was picking out a melody on an imaginary keyboard, I said, 'Right, tomorrow morning we're going to Buenos Aires to buy a piano.'

Good ones cost a fortune, and we were scraping to buy bricks to build a house. We ended up at a pawnshop somewhere around the Plaza Once and there, in the darkest corner, was the little piano – it was barely a piano at all but more of a spinet – and, because its strings had few notes left in them, it cost only thirty thousand pesos, or the same as a couple of thousand bricks. So we bought it for temporary use, and as soon as the Krämer arrived we'd sell this one; if nobody wanted it we'd give it away, and Bob's your uncle.

Our new piano was sent to us by rail, in high summer. Eight-hundred-odd miles shut up in a goods van, *click-clack*ing over worn sleepers in the suffocating heat of the arid plains was a risky proposition for our instrument, which, fondly, we began to call Pérez. That way, from the

[203]

very outset, the astronomical differences between the two pianos would be clear from their names.

Normally Pérez would have arrived in three days, but the train got caught up in the first summer floods, a yearly event that washed away stretches of track at Cruz del Eje, and there was a delay until another train could bring rails and sleepers to reroute the line. So Pérez got to us several days late, without a packing crate, wrapped in brown paper and some dirty cardboard tied up with rough twine – a disaster, out of tune, and with quite a few wobbly hammers. On the keyboard cover, stuck down with tape, was a tuning peg. When we bought the piano we hadn't been told it would not hold its pitch for long, but they'd been good enough to send us a peg.

The piano occupied the place reserved for the Krämer (not completely, it was smaller) or, rather, we lent the space to the new piano, since it was always meant to be provisional. We cleaned it inside and out (it came with two filthy spoons, whose connection with a piano was pure Buñuel). After seeing the ruinous state of its frame, its worn wrest-pins, and its frayed strings, we decided to tune it initially to a rather low A, like Verdi's, of 432 vibrations per second, which was even a bit lower than my violin, but the Pérez seemed to breathe better.

We launched our piano with Corelli's 'La Follia'. And it sounded wonderful. Pérez seemed to have been built for the piece, for it gave him the chance to do himself full justice. The instrument seemed to know the Corelli by heart and, according to Irma, to be playing the piece all by itself, as if Pérez had it stored inside him, hidden among his strings. Because you only had to touch the keys of the first chord for its old hull to creak, for its sails to unfurl, and for it to take off with the wind behind it.

A month's work, six hours a day, and my fingers memorized the Corelli sonata in the same way that little Pérez had it imprinted in his strings. And one fine morning (as in the poem about Martín Fierro, when he and Cruz cross the last frontier), Irma and I left home and went down Rivadavia towards the Conservatoire to play in the competition.

The jury, all of whom had come from Buenos Aires – that is, practically Europe – were awful. I have no idea what they thought of us but when I said that with my wife as my accompanist I was going to play 'La Follia', one of them remarked, 'Isn't that a very difficult piece?'

The brand-new Conservatoire's piano, a Gaveau baby grand, sounded like two Pérezes put together. You have no idea how I had to struggle with my A string. The piano must have been tuned not to everyone else's 440 but to 456, according to the latest trends transported secretly from Germany. Thank goodness neither Irma nor I had to sing, otherwise we would have lost our voices. The winner was my little violin, which, instead of being mass produced by a cut-rate joiner, seemed a violin crafted by some luthier of renown. We won the competition, of course – that is, I won the right to become a member of the Conservatoire's permanent string quartet, which was in the process of being formed, and of its forthcoming chamber orchestra.

Carlos Cáceres had intended it to be a string quartet, but as no viola came forward, we invited Edith Fernández, a pianist, to join us, so making the group a *Klavier Quarttet*. First violin, Chicho Palmieri; second, yours truly; cello, Celestino Palmieri; and, on the Gaveau, Edith, surrounded by the halo of having been a pupil of Scaramuzza and companion of Marta Argerich. The group allowed us to exalt Beethoven's Piano Quartet, Opus 16, which we played in every village and town of La Rioja, which for hundreds of years had been musically isolated. Even though audiences seemed to have forgotten the piece, owing to a dearth of quartets, sure enough, on scratching a little deeper, we found the work perfectly preserved for happier times in the collective musical unconscious.

Be that as it may, to get back to little Pérez, whom we sometimes called *Kleine Pérez* to help him cope with his humbleness, it became clearer with each passing day that we had to replace him, for he no longer could even hold Verdi's A. We had to move on, to look good, to play more difficult works, and he was not up to it. The only piece in which he sounded fine was 'La Follia'; in everything else he was utter disaster.

Irma and I made up our minds to get rid of him, but at the same time it hurt us when he sang with only half a voice (his lungs were no longer up to it). It seemed to us that, knowing we wanted to abandon him to his fate, he took pains to stay tuned for a whole week. As a result of his efforts he became even more out of tune and, what was worse, all of a sudden – as if overcome by a fit of coughing. He wanted to stay with us for ever, but his health was no longer good enough.

Every time a lorry's brakes screeched on the corner outside, the little piano's heart seemed to thump in fright, as if he thought the noise was the vehicle at long last delivering the Krämer which he so dreaded, for it would mean his disappearance or removal to a piano cemetery, a place that does not even exist. Then his corpse, like Paganini's, excommunicated by the pope for making pacts with the devil, would not even lie in hallowed ground. That's why Pérez trembled (as did Irma and I) every time he heard the sound of a lorry.

So as not to have to sell him, we began lending him out. A few hours or days away from us made us value him more. Absence makes the heart grow fonder. It was pointless trying to tune him to the 440 A that customers demanded.

He would not even hold his pitch for half an hour. So we left him more or less where he wanted, close to but not quite at Verdi's 432. But he couldn't even hold that, and every so often you had to raise the pitch of his strings with the peg.

Changing singers' voices by his pitch, he ruined some established reputations and wrecked the careers of several quite promising folk singers. Without knowing why, they began singing outside their registers, nor had they any idea why audiences whistled and jeered and, as if that were not enough, threw rotten cactus fruit at them.

Even Peggy Collins, the only singer from La Rioja with an English name, refused to be accompanied by our little Pérez when performing the song she knew best, the one where 'les filles de Paris' come in. One night, in spite of radio publicity and an assembled audience, her concert was called off. The moment she appeared on stage, ready to make her bow, and saw Pérez awaiting her she fled without a word. Some people applauded – for what reason, who can say? At which, Pérez became the only piano that instead of accompanying a singer actually silenced her.

Luis Barrera, a friend of ours, a door-to-door salesman with a small van, one day said, 'That little piano sounds bad because you two have never valued it. You look down on it, waiting for the other piano to arrive. Pérez needs someone to look after him and appreciate him. He deserves it. Why don't you sell him to me?'

The day he took Pérez away gave us a twinge of regret, but we at once put it out of mind because we had reason to believe that the Krämer would soon be with us.

Barrera, who had a nose for business, got hold of a lumbering old dray, drawn by a pair of horses, and mounted the piano on it, hiring out the contraption to young men who went serenading in the evening streets, taking advantage of a government decree that supported musical activity of this sort, which was deeply rooted in old La Rioja traditions. Rolling along on car tyres, the wagon barely made a sound, which was ideal for night work, since it did not disturb the neighbours. It had a folding aluminium canopy in case it rained unexpectedly. With his soft tone and his worn hammers, which sort of hit sideways, as if plucking the strings instead of striking them, Pérez sounded like a baroque guitar, and this delighted both the serenaders and their female followers.

As a result, however, Pérez lost a bit of his identity. Of his bulk only his keyboard was visible. It was built into the wagon, forming part of the coachwork – or, rather, it was the coachwork, but a musical one. This was the piano's first humiliation. When the serenades went out of fashion, Barrera rented the dray as a comic attraction to the small circuses without animals or clowns that dared venture to those north-western solitudes; but when people heard Pérez, instead of laughing they wept.

From then on, so worn were his strings that the little piano spoke rather than sang. When the more or less sporadic economic crises became permanent, the circuses struck La Rioja off their itineraries. Barrera put his contraption up for sale, and little Pérez was acquired by a businessman from the nearby village of Sanagasta, where the piano was taken under his own steam – that is, drawn by a pair of horses across twenty miles of stony ground, which left his strings in an even worse state. The local folk singers, who had no idea how to use a piano's keys, regarded Pérez purely as percussion and used him as a drum, hitting him anywhere; and, because by that time he was very old and nothing could hurt him any longer, Pérez put up with it all.

When he stopped being a novelty, his new owner turned

him into a countertop. People drank leaning on a bar that at the same time played popular folk tunes. Pérez's parched wood absorbed the wine that sloshed from the glasses, and when he got drunk, instead of folk songs he'd come out with 'La Follia', which was his pride and joy. But people did not like this and made him shut up.

And so, eventually, March 1976 came round, and Argentina was once more saddled with a military dictatorship. If we wanted to go on living, Irma and I had twenty-four hours in which to leave La Rioja and head for Spain. We packed up the house and when we reached the provincial border, near Córdoba, half lulled to sleep by the silence of the desert and the dark years that were gathering, a lorry suddenly overtook us on its way to the humid pampa, carrying in a crate made out of European Christmas tree no less than the mythological Krämer, which, unable to find its addressee, was returning not in sorrow or in triumph to an uncertain future.

In the course of that future, for lack of anyone to play it, the piano became a decoration. The keys filled with an encrusted deposit, oblivion invaded it, and consequently it contracted the most terrible of viruses – silence. Tiring of it, the piano's owners swapped it with a neighbour for a colour television. On the humid pampa fighting the damp patches on the walls of old houses is an unequal struggle. The Krämer was not in fact acquired for playing (no one in the house knew how) but for hiding a huge stain on the living-room wall, which the television had not been able to conceal. The piano was completely covered with a large white rug, on which 'Krämer' was embroidered in blue silk, except for the ¨ over the *a*, which was picked out in red. We heard that on some Christmases its owners had tried to open it, to raise the lid of the keyboard, but it was firmly seized up with the calcified impurities in the keys and the implacable mildew of time. So that the white rug that covered it turned into its sudarium.

In Madrid the years began to pass, and one day the postman handed me a big fat envelope containing a score, with a barely legible handwritten explanation saying something like 'This is a zamba the lads wrote for little Pérez.'

The lyrics disclosed our piano's finale. Pérez was primed to play folk music, but, stubbornly, in the middle of a piece he would introduce chords from Corelli, because certain passages of 'La Follia' still thrilled him. The audience, who knew nothing of Corelli, thought they were mistakes. He, meanwhile, was trying to give of his best. His last owners, hearing him pitch his voice to these passages, decided that Pérez was ready for the knacker's.

According to the lyrics, while being taken in the back of a wagon to be chopped up into firewood for a barbecue, his timbers began to play, trying hard to sketch the melody of 'La Follia'. But he never got beyond the first three or four notes. He kept repeating them, each time more slowly, more faintly, until he fell mute, as if he had wound down, which is what happens to musical boxes.

MEN, THOSE FABULOUS CREATURES

A.L. Barker

'This is the Garden Room, Mrs Wyvern,' said the Matron, 'where we keep the perennials. It gets the best of the sun and it's handy for the toilet.'

'Wyvern-Chilmondham.'

'Honey, that's a nice name but they can't manage double-barrels. And if I introduce you by your initials it's going to be Mrs W.C.' She laughed. 'We'll call you Mrs Why.'

I had made allowances for her, I always make allowances for persons unknown, but I was finding her displeasing. For one thing, she was too young. I judged her to be in her early twenties: pert, with the brash good looks common to people of a certain class. I would have allowed her her youth, which is not shameful, had she shown a modicum of sensibility about her position as Matron of a Residential Home for the Elderly.

'Now where would you like to start? With our oldest inhabitant, or our baby – she's eighty-six and blows bubbles.'

'I should like to take off my hat and coat.' The room was disagreeably warm and I was wearing my silver fox cape.

'Don't leave that lying around,' she said. 'It's the sort of thing they love.'

'I thought it might lead to a little talk about wildlife and ecology. What are they interested in?' I was anticipating stringent limitations because none of these people seemed concerned enough even to adjust the television which was showing orange faces and rolling.

'Oh, everything!' said this Matron. 'Tell me what you're

[213]

interested in and I'll point you to someone who can talk about it.'

'I am here to talk to them.'

'You'll be lucky to get a word in edgeways!'

It was ungracious, to say the least, since I had sacrificed time and inclination to bring to these terminally old a breath of the outside world.

'I must warn you we have some quirky types here. Mrs O'Halloran's grandson taught her the karate chop and she'll practise on you if she gets half a chance. One of my male nurses was off for a week after he bent down to pick up her knitting. Dick Vogeler thinks he's the Earl of Leicester and I'm Queen Elizabeth the First.' She giggled. 'It gets quite sticky at times. There's an old fellow who was in the Navy and thinks we're a ship at sea – '

'That might be a point of contact. My husband was at the Admiralty.'

'He swabs his room with the O'Cedar mop every morning. Melanie Gosschalk keeps a gin bottle filled with tapwater and gets high on it. I bet you're wishing you hadn't come!'

'I'm here to talk to them and talk I shall.'

Someone waved from the far side of the room. 'Then there's Henry – I'll have to leave you to it, dear, we have a crisis upstairs, it's Mrs Treadgold's bathtime.'

So I was left in their midst. I saw what she had meant by 'perennials'. They *looked* permanent, ranged round the walls in wheel- or armchairs, arrayed in bright colours, blue, red, yellow cardigans and shawls, green and pink check carpet slippers, like a herbaceous border. Some had their eyes shut, some watched me through slits. I slipped off my fox cape and stroked it for comfort. How absurd that I should feel the need!

Where to start was the lesser of my problems, for there

would be nowhere to sit when I did; I'd be obliged to hover or crouch beside one or other of them to make myself understood.

My husband's last words to me had been, 'Remember, they won't know you from Adam,' an admonition I had felt disposed to ignore. Mine is an established reputation as a public woman. My name features on committees for the promotion of the rights of housewives, the provision of facilities for nursing mothers on buses and in the Tube, the preservation of local monuments and open spaces. In many households my name is a household word. Ignorance is omission, not advantage. If these people did not know me, I should make myself known.

The person who had waved now crooked a finger and wagged it. I crossed the room in what would have been a deadly hush but for the television which was holding up a bank with machine guns.

He was a nice-looking old man with a smooth skin and a mop of silvery hair. I said, 'Good morning. How are you?'

'Potbound. She calls us perennials but I'm a softy annual. Shan't last another year.'

He was well wrapped up in that overheated room: a mohair shawl about his shoulders and a travelling rug over his legs and feet. But his lips were mauve and there was a network of blue veins across his temple.

'One must think positive,' I said.

'Positivity's been my problem. Sit down and I'll tell you why.'

'There's nowhere to sit.'

'There's the floor.'

'I can't . . .'

'Why not? You're well upholstered.'

'I prefer to stand.'

'It hurts my neck to keep craning to look up at you.'

[215]

His skinny neck was indeed rigid; a shadowing, like the cracks in fine china, had appeared in his face. I looked round: there wasn't a vacant chair and hardly space to put a pin between the occupied ones. Gingerly, I let myself sink to the floor. The television fell briefly silent; I heard a throaty murmur go round the room.

'That's better,' he said, 'now we can talk.'

'I don't know if you've seen the papers this morning. The situation in the Baltic is quite unprecedented – '

'I don't read newspapers, they're all sex.'

'That scarcely applies to the demise of the Communist regime.'

'Are you a woman of the world?'

I said my interests were wide, I might say universal, the galactic system especially appealed to me.

'I was afraid you'd rabbit on about your grandchildren.'

'I have no grandchildren.'

To my surprise and annoyance he patted me on the head, on my hat which I had not removed. 'I can't stand women who are wrapped up in babies.'

'If you are referring to the so-called maternal instinct, a merely biological function, I should point out that I am President of an international committee which provides assistance to orphans of the Third World and grants to single parent families in the United Kingdom.'

'Thy servant, a woman. You know how that started – she dried a man's feet on her hair.'

'Surely that was an act of religious devotion!'

'Oh my.' He sighed. 'I was born into a household of women: my mother, a cook-housekeeper and a girl to take care of me. My father was a trapper, he vanished into the African jungle and was presumed dead – my mother presumed it. She used to make me stand in his shoes, size eleven, and she'd cry, "He was such a big man!"'

'What did he trap?'

'Elephants, for ivory.'

I admit to thinking that a man who followed such a trade was expendable.

'One of them trod on him. The natives patched him up but wouldn't let him go. They made him head trapper, gave him a hut, a share of the ivory and he could take what he liked of the communal wives.'

'How interesting.'

'Nice while it lasted. Then the supply of elephants ran out and we got a wire, "Coming home, Father". It was deeply significant. I was only four years old and didn't know what it signified, but she knew.' He chuckled. 'My mother knew.'

I glanced at the television which was canonising a packet of breakfast cereal.

'Remember,' he said, tapping me on my collarbone, 'my father had never seen me, he disappeared before I was born, all he had to go on was her suspicion that she might be pregnant. I could have been a false alarm. Yet he signed himself "Father".'

'He was living in hope all those years in the jungle.'

'He'd made up his mind. Fortunately for my mother, when he landed at Southampton he had to go straight into hospital with an attack of malaria. She went to visit him. Young as I was, I could see she was frightened and when she came back from the hospital she was distracted. My nursemaid, Pollyanna, asked was he really so bad. No, said my mother, he would soon be able to come home. Then they went up to my mother's room and talked. I hung about outside, I heard Pollyanna laugh, but my mother didn't.

'Next day she told me I was to have new clothes for when Father came home. Pollyanna said, "You can't keep it up for ever!" and my mother said, "Only until he gets to know

[217]

and love the child. Promise you won't give me away!" "I won't," said Pollyanna, "but Cook might. You'll have to get rid of her. And there are the tradespeople." My mother said my father didn't talk to tradespeople.'

'What precisely was it that she wasn't going to keep up?'

'You'll have to wait for the end of the story.'

'There is a story?'

He nudged me with his foot. 'You bet! My mother bought me a blue suit with long trousers and brass buttons. I fancied myself in it. Then she took me to the hospital to visit my father. He was very big, his feet hung out of the end of his bed. I strutted to and fro showing off my new suit. He called me to him and smacked my bottom hard. I cried, he yelled at me to handle myself like a man. There was quite a scene, he demanded to know what my mother thought she was doing to his son. "I give you a son," he kept saying, "and you're making him a little queen."

'I decided I didn't like him. I told him, "I'm not yours, I'm hers," and clung to my mother. He turned green and shook so violently that his bedstead rattled. Mother had to call a nurse who stuck a needle in his arm. He gave me a toy boat and went to sleep.

'Mother sent our cook-housekeeper away. Pollyanna was bad at cooking and at making the beds and sweeping. Everything got dusty and we got hard potatoes and lumpy rice to eat.

'Mother tried to teach Pollyanna to make a steak and kidney pie which was my father's favourite. She was looking really scared, she would stand at the window, watching the road. When I asked what she was waiting for, she cried, "Nothing!" She was waiting for my father.

'The day he came home Pollyanna served up a meat pudding without any meat in it and a custard tart with a skin like a rhinoceros. He told Mother to get rid of her.

Mother said she couldn't. He got up from the table and went straight out to the kitchen. Mother wept into her plate. When Pollyanna came to clear away the dishes she begged her to take no notice of him. "Oh, but I have," said Pollyanna. "I've taken a week's notice." "Please, please say you won't tell him!" Pollyanna smiled sweetly. "I won't tell him." My mother threw her arms round Pollyanna's neck and kissed her.'

'Tell him what?' I said irritably, aware how ridiculous I must look, sitting at this man's feet as if he was a guru.

'She didn't have to.' His smile was far from sweet. 'When my father came up to my nursery and saw my toys, my teddy-bears and rabbits – I loved cuddly things – he was furious. "A son of mine, playing with dolls!" I had a dolls' house, he put his fist through the roof. I was too astonished even to cry.

'Pollyanna said, "He may want to be an architect." "He'll go to sea," said my father. "The sea will make a man or a shark's dinner of him!" "In that case," said Pollyanna, "come and see him sail his boat in his bath," and she began to undress me.'

He sat back in his chair, but not before he had poked me in the ribs. The television was making us morally responsible for the famine in Ethiopia, showing selective shots of skeletal babies and women scratching in the dust.

'My husband was at the Admiralty,' I said.

Just then the Matron returned, bustling up as I was endeavouring to stretch my legs which had been in hairpin bends for too long. 'How are you getting on, Mrs Why?'

'I have been listening to a story.' I turned to the old man. 'You haven't finished it, I am still waiting to know what your mother couldn't tell your father.'

He tapped the side of his nose in a gesture of secrecy. 'I once heard her talking about "the absence of a head of the

house". I asked what the head of a house was and she said
"A man."'

'Now, Henry,' said the Matron, 'it's time for your consti-
tutional.' She flung back the rug from his knees. I saw that
he was wearing a skirt and black woollen stockings.

'Henry?' I said.

'Henrietta Shaw-Babington, she's a double-barrel, like
you.'

BIOGRAPHICAL NOTES

CLARE COLVIN makes her sixth appearance in *Winter's Tales*. Her stories have been translated and adapted for radio. She has recently completed a collection and is working on a novel. Born in London, she has worked as a journalist in various fields, from political and foreign reporting to drama criticism, and is now Literary Editor of the *Sunday Express*.

ROBERT EDRIC was born in Sheffield in 1956. He has published seven novels, including *Winter Garden* (1985), winner of the James Tait Black Memorial Award, and *A New Ice Age* (1986), runner-up for the Guardian Fiction Prize. His most recent book is *The Earth Made of Glass*.

KETO VON WABERER was born in Augsburg, Germany. She has lived in Mexico and the United States and now resides in Munich. She has published several collections of short stories and a novel. She writes for various German newspapers, including *Die Ziet* and *Die Woche*.

JAMIE O'NEILL lives and works in London. His second novel, *Kilbrack, or Who is Nancy Valentine?* was published in 1990. Brought up in Dún Laoghaire, Co Dublin, where the mailboats leave for England, he is Irish, and was born in 1961. This is his second appearance in *Winter's Tales*.

TONY PEAKE was born in South Africa in 1951. He now lives in London, where he works as a literary agent. He has been a previous contributor to *Winter's Tales*, and his work also appears in the *Penguin Book of Contemporary South African Stories*. His first novel, *A Summer Tide*, is published by Abacus. He has edited a collection of stories on the theme of seduction for Serpent's Tail. He is currently working on his second novel, and the authorised biography of Derek Jarman.

RONALD FRAME was born in 1953 in Glasgow, and educated there and at Oxford. He is the author of award-winning television and radio plays.

[221]

His eleventh book of fiction was published in the Spring. A television memoir, called *Ghost City*, was broadcast in September.

JUAN FORN, who was born in Buenos Aires in 1959, is the author of the novel *Corazones cautivos más arriba* (1987) and the short stories *Nadar ne noche* (1991), from which the present story is drawn. This is his third appearance in *Winter's Tales*. Currently finishing a new novel, he is Editor-in-Chief at Editorial Planeta, in Argentina.

PHILIP MACCANN was born in England and moved to Ireland at an early age. He reviews fiction occasionally for the *Guardian*. His first collection of short stories is published in January. His stories have appeared in *New Writing* 1 and 3 (Minerva), *Winter's Tales 9* and Faber's *First Fictions 11*.

TOM WAKEFIELD was born into a mining family in the Midlands. He now lives in London. Among his many successful novels are *Mates*, *The Discus Throwers*, *The Variety Artistes*, *Lot's Wife* and *War Paint*. His novella, *The Other Way*, was published by Constable in 1992 in the collection *Secret Lives*.

MONICA FURLONG is a biographer and novelist. Her biographies include *Merton* (1980), *Genuine Fake* (1986) and *Therese of Lisieux* (1987, for Virago). Her novels are *The Cat's Eye* (1976), *Cousins* (1983) and *Wise Child* (1987).

DANIEL MOYANO published six novels and six short story collections in his lifetime. Born in Buenos Aires in 1930, he worked as a journalist and as a music teacher in La Rioja, in the poor northwest corner of Argentina. Jailed briefly by the military authorities in 1976, he left the country and settled with his family in Spain, where in 1981 he became a Spanish citizen. Upon his death, in Madrid, in 1992, he left his last novel and a final collection of short fiction. His story here, from this volume, is as yet unpublished in Spanish. A novel, *The Devil's Trill*, was published in London, in 1988; another, *The Flight of the Tiger*, will appear shortly.

A. L. BARKER left school when she was sixteen and, after the war, joined the BBC. Her debut collection of short stories, *Innocents*, won the Somerset Maugham Prize, and her novel *John Brown's Body* was shortlisted for the Booker Prize in 1969. She is the author of ten novels and many more short stories, her preferred form. She is a Fellow of the Royal Society of Literature and of P.E.N.